Invisible World

Invisible World

A NOVEL OF THE SALEM WITCH TRIALS

SUZANNE WEYN

SCHOLASTIC PRESS/NEW YORK

Library of Congress Cataloging-in-Publication Data available

ISBN 978-0-545-33486-0

10 9 8 7 6 5 4 3 2 1   12 13 14 15 16

Printed in the U.S.A.   23

First edition, August 2012

The text was set in Diotima.

Book design by Kristina Iulo

With thanks to Bill Gonzalez for your research help, suggestions, and unflagging enthusiasm; to David M. Young for your unfailing and generous willingness to always brainstorm with me; and to David Levithan for being the best, most supportive, and brilliant editor on the planet.

"I cannot help it; the Devil may appear in my shape."

REBECCA NURSE, 1692

Hung for witchcraft

"The black dog said 'Serve me,' but I said I am afraid.
He said if I did not, he would do worse to me."

TITUBA THE SLAVE, 1692

Confessed to using witchcraft

FROM THE ORIGINAL TRANSCRIPTS OF THE SALEM WITCH TRIALS, 1692

Prologue

EVERY TIME THE GUARD ARRIVES, IT IS AN EXCITEMENT. THE moment his keys jangle in the door lock, my fifty or so cell mates stir excitedly, roused from their listless despair. Filthy hair is tossed back. Sleepy eyes are rubbed clear.

The guard is very tall, with a starkly pale face. On these patrols, he does not wear the metal helmet that reminds me of a horseshoe crab. His musket remains holstered at the side of his doublet. He is not fearful of us captive women.

Or that's what he wants us to believe, at any rate.

He's revolted by the stench of body odor and spoiled food that greets him. With raised chin, he makes no effort to conceal his contempt.

A few women plead on bended knees, arms outstretched.

"My husband cannot look after the children and also tend the harvest. Our crops are withering."

"I'm told my baby is ill. Release me, I beg you."

"I have done nothing wrong! Please!"

One woman assaults him with logic. "Why would I kill

Goodwife Smith's cow? I simply complained that her milk was becoming too expensive. That doesn't mean I wish her — or her cow — any ill. I need the milk that the Smiths sell. How can they accuse me of killing the cow with evil spells? *I don't even know what a spell sounds like.* This is not right. I demand to be let go."

The slave woman Tituba sleeps shackled in the corner, dreaming of her little girl, Violet. They are in the rye field behind the house, playing among the rustling stalks. I know this because her dream thoughts are vivid and flow easily into my clairvoyant mind. I am grateful that she is not recalling the terrifying episodes of demonic possession that put her here.

These women are innocent. I'm sure of it. Yet — innocent or not — in the coming days they will dangle from the hangman's noose on Gallows Hill. Seventeen have been executed already. One man, Giles Corey, was crushed to death. Two have died in jail.

Four-year-old Dorcas Good looks at me, big-eyed and scared, from across our cell. The demonic thing running rampant through Salem has not even spared this child.

Dorcas begins to sob pitifully and I cross to her side, rubbing her skinny shoulders as she whimpers into my skirt. The guard, clearly unnerved, hurries through the door, locks it, and disappears.

The pleading women slump to the ground, as though the guard has taken their last sparks with him. No more arguments are voiced once he's gone.

I lean back against the wall. After fifteen or so minutes, voices enter my head, as they always do in the moments just before I drift off to the distant shore of sleep. I can hear my cell mates thinking.

I have always been able to hear the thoughts of others. Not just imagine them. Really hear them inside my head.

Tom must get word to Uncle James. He can help.

I am so scared. I don't want to hang.

My baby will die without me.

It is driving me insane.

I focus on a memory that helps me shut out the voices; I try to see it in my mind's eye as clearly as possible. *It is spring. I am beside a forsythia bush; its flowers have already burst open in shades of fiery yellow. My sister is there. We are about to crawl into an opening in the bush, to its dark center.*

The other women's voices are blocked by my memory's images and no longer plague me.

Instead, it is my own voice that warns me. My own voice that expresses fear.

I try to sleep. But sleep won't come.

There is too much to worry about.

Will the evil come back for me?

It might.

The hideous, demonic creature that I have let loose on Salem Village might not be through with me yet.

Chapter One

SUSSEX, ENGLAND, 1681

*I*N MY EARLIEST MEMORY, I AM SIX AND MY OLDER SISTER, Kate, is nine. We had crawled to the center of the wide-spreading forsythia bush at the rear of our manor house. At that time, it was my favorite place on earth.

Through the lemony umbrella of petals, dappled sunlight played over the loose, dark soil. The flowers had no scent, but the branches, moist with sticky sap, enlivened the air with a woodsy greenness.

When Kate tossed back her luxurious dark curls, I saw her smooth cheek was speckled with dirt. The lace collar of her blue brocade gown had become rumpled and dotted with the soil she had been digging with her hands.

"I'm ready to bury him," Kate said in a low, solemn voice. "Please hand me the bird, Elsabeth."

Striving to match her dignity, I unfolded the embroidered handkerchief on my lap and lifted the lifeless body of a wren. I couldn't resist tenderly stroking its soft chest.

We had buried several birds, a garden snake, and even a few of the mice our black cat loved to kill, here in our secret animal burial ground. The largest inhabitant of our graveyard was an exquisite red fox that Kate and I had found while walking in the woods that past winter.

"We should pray for the bird's soul," Kate suggested. "But first we need to cover him with dirt."

I dug my hands into the loosened earth Kate had piled into a mound and began to assist her. As we worked, I plucked up a large rock embedded in the dirt and discovered a world of insects living beneath: larvae, beetles, spiders, worms. They scurried off for safety, alarmed at being so abruptly uncovered.

"Ew! Bugs!" Kate said, recoiling in disgust.

I didn't feel the same. To me, insects were fascinating. And it was amazing to think that a whole world of them existed right there under a rock, just waiting to be discovered. I wondered what their lives could be like. Did they love each other as people did? Were they upset to have their rock taken away just as I would be if I had to leave my home?

"Do birds and bugs have souls, do you think?" I questioned.

"They must," Kate replied. "Doesn't every living thing?"

Raising my chin, I gazed around the sun-specked cathedral of nature in which we knelt. "Plants are alive," I said. "Do *they* have souls?"

Kate frowned, considering the question. "I don't know. But surely animals must have souls."

"Do you think this bird will go to animal Heaven?" I probed.

"Yes. Animals must have a separate Heaven for themselves."

This idea struck me as quite awful. "I hope animals and plants and even bugs all go to *regular* people Heaven," I insisted fervently.

I returned to the job of tossing dirt into the bird's little grave. Suddenly, though, I lifted my head, listening sharply.

I'd heard a voice. But had it come from the outside world or was it speaking from within my mind?

I grabbed Kate's wrist in alarm. "Bronwyn is looking for us," I said. In my head, I could hear our governess calling.

With my fingers still encircling my sister's wrist, we both closed our eyes and listened again, turning inward.

Now where are those girls? I told them not to wander off.

Bronwyn had one of those minds — clear and focused — that we had no trouble reading. Plus, she had been our governess since I was born. My mother had died in the process of giving birth to me, and Bronwyn was all I had ever known of motherly love.

"Hurry," Kate urged.

"Out of there this instant, you naughty girls!"

"Bronwyn, is that you?" I asked, stalling for time as we filled in the grave.

"You know who it is! Now come out of there, I say!"

Quickly patting down the dirt mound above our dead bird friend, I stripped a handful of yellow flowers from their stalks and tossed them on the grave. Then I crawled out the opening in the branches that Kate and I used as a door. Kate followed.

Bronwyn stood waiting, arms folded, right hip jutting to the side, her lined, fine-boned face pulled into an expression of sternness. The day had turned gray and Bronwyn's salt-and-pepper hair danced at her cheekbones where the wind had pried it from its simple arrangement. "Didn't I tell you to stay by the back door while I supervised the hanging of the bedsheets?" she scolded.

Nearly a quarter acre of rolling lawn stood between us and the stone manor house. Kate and I had wild, uncultivated woods to our backs and the ocean just beyond that. "Sorry, Bronwyn, we —" Kate began.

"And what mischief have you two been up to?" Bronwyn demanded, brushing the dirt from Kate's cheek.

"We found a bird," Kate answered, as though this were a perfectly adequate excuse for tiring of our game of hide-and-seek between the billowing sheets and wandering off. "A dead bird."

A light rain suddenly moistened my face. "Bronwyn, could we sing a song for the bird we just buried?" I asked.

"It should have a burial song," Kate agreed. "Could you sing it, Bronwyn? Your voice is so lovely."

Bronwyn checked the sky, rain misting her. "Perhaps a *quick* song," she allowed with some reluctance. She reached her hands to us and we each took hold. Bronwyn began a song that neither Kate nor I could understand, for she sang it in the Scottish dialect of her home in the north. It was beautiful and moving, nonetheless.

"What do the words mean?" Kate asked when Bronwyn had finished.

"It was a song for the death of an animal. My granny taught it to me," Bronwyn replied. "It wishes the animal well on its way to the other side."

"The other side of what?" Kate asked.

"The other side of the veil."

"The veil?"

"The veil is lifted from time to time to reveal realms that lie beyond what can be seen here on this plane of existence, the worlds beyond our knowing, the invisible world." That Bronwyn had some mysterious acquaintance with this realm had never been in doubt to me.

"As in Heaven?" Kate asked.

"Heaven means many different things to many different people," Bronwyn answered. "But yes, it could be considered a world behind the veil."

The rain began to fall more heavily. Bronwyn grabbed my hand and Kate's and we walked toward the house.

"Next time don't touch a hurt animal. Come to get me first," Bronwyn instructed us, not for the first time.

We had brought Bronwyn injured animals before and knew that she had a box of ointments, salves, herbs, and oils that she kept under her bed. After consulting a thick and ancient-looking book, she would mix these together in different combinations and either administer the concoction by mouth or slather it onto the skin of the hurt creature. Sometimes the animal died anyway, but more often it was healed.

Bronwyn often told us of her girlhood in Scotland, spent in a rural village that was still steeped in ancient ways from the old times. She'd lived in a thatched cottage with her many sisters, aunts, and cousins, as well as a grandmother who was so far on in years that no one — not even the grandmother herself — knew her age. It was believed that she was well over one hundred! Bronwyn claimed that it was this old granny that everyone in

the village turned to in times of sickness and injury. It w
her that Bronwyn had learned all her healing arts.

Kate and I thought of Bronwyn as a sort of wizard, a genius,
and wanted to tell everyone about her skill, but she warned us
against uttering a word. Her light eyes clouded over when she
commanded us to keep silent. "You must swear to me that you
will never tell a soul of this. Swear! You could put me in the
greatest peril if you reveal what I do for these animals. I am a fool
to do it."

"We won't ever tell," Kate swore as I nodded vigorously at
her side.

We were full of promises, back then.

Chapter Two

WHEN WE ARRIVED AT THE MANOR HOUSE, THREE MAIDS were already pulling in the bedding. Bronwyn continued on, leading us into the kitchen and steering us toward the blazing hearth. She perched on its stone rim and grabbed a white towel from the pile neatly folded on a nearby table. She fluffed the tops of our hair dry, careful not to undo Kate's tight curls, less so with my free-flowing brown waves.

A servant, pretty young Elyn, met us by the fire. "Sir Alexander would like to see the girls right now," she told Bronwyn.

"For more testing?" Bronwyn asked, pulling us closer to her.

Elyn nodded. "I believe so. He wants to see them in his laboratory. He sent me to fetch them."

"Very well," Bronwyn told Elyn. "Then after that, if this rain lets up and it's not too chilly, we will start our swimming lessons at the shore. You can't be living at the ocean shore and not know how to swim. It's too dangerous."

Kate and I looked at each other, our eyes lit with enthusiasm. To learn to swim! We were so lucky to have Bronwyn as our governess.

"Now go with Elyn, girls, and do well for your father," Bronwyn said, releasing us from the encircling protection of her arms.

Alarm filled Kate's eyes. "I don't want to," she pleaded with Bronwyn. "Please don't make us go."

Bronwyn stroked Kate's dark curls kindly. "It's not up to me, pet. Your father is a scientist and he's researching the family power. You girls both possess it."

"But it frightens me," Kate insisted.

Bronwyn knelt so that her face was on level with ours. "I understand that it seems strange to you sometimes, and I worry that it strains your young minds. But there is nothing to fear, girls. It's not a bad or an evil thing. Your grandmother from Scotland on your father's side had the power. She was a gifted clairvoyant, a mind reader of such power that many people came to see her to learn of the future."

"She knew the future?" I was impressed.

Bronwyn nodded knowingly. "She was a mind reader and could also predict upcoming events."

Gooseflesh formed on my arms. I felt chills of excitement. "How do you know about this?" I asked.

"As you know, your dear late mother was my good friend. She told me." Bronwyn lowered her head and spoke on in a quiet, conspiratorial tone. "Your grandmother's mother before her was also a gifted dream interpreter and could see the future. A queen once consulted your great-grandmother."

"What queen?" Kate asked in a breathless whisper, her fears momentarily eclipsed by her excitement.

"Mary, Queen of Scots," Bronwyn confided, lowering her voice even further so the kitchen staff wouldn't hear. Kate and I drew very close. "The queen dreamt she saw a head floating in the air and was directed by her advisors to see your great-grandmother to find out what it meant. She felt it was an important dream."

"What did our great-grandmother tell her?" I asked.

"She told Queen Mary that her head would soon be chopped off!" Bronwyn replied dramatically.

Kate and I gasped. "I bet the queen didn't like to hear that," I ventured.

"She did not," Bronwyn confirmed. "During one of the several Scottish witch crazes, she made sure your great-gran was burned as a witch."

"Burned?" Kate asked, shaken with horror. "While she was alive?"

Bronwyn nodded. "What an awful way to die, eh? It made people practice the old ways in secret, for fear of being hunted for witchcraft. But the more secretive people became, the worse it looked for them when they were discovered."

"And was great-gran right?" Kate asked. "About Queen Mary, I mean?"

Bronwyn nodded solemnly. "Mary Stuart was beheaded for plotting to murder her cousin Queen Elizabeth."

"Did they think Mary was a witch?" I inquired, trying to understand the logic behind all this, if indeed there was any.

"No, just bad and disloyal," Bronwyn replied.

This made no sense to me. Our great-grandmother, who had been good and helpful, was killed just the same as a queen who was nearly a murderess.

"Why has Father never told us of our grandmother and great-grandmother?" Kate asked. "We've never heard of them."

"He doesn't like to talk about it," Bronwyn told us.

"I forgot something," I lied, backing toward the door. Turning, I ran for the outside. "I'll be right back!" I shouted over my shoulder.

It was still raining lightly, and I loved the feel of wet grass under my bare feet. Where was I headed? I didn't know. But I had to get out of that house and out into the open so I could think my dangerous thoughts alone.

When I got as far as the wide forsythia bush, I slowed, panting. "Little bird! Little bird! Let your spirit rise up!" I shouted, raising my arms skyward. "Fly beyond the veil!"

Something chirped.

A bird — exactly like the one we'd just buried — sat atop the forsythia, looking directly at me. I shut my eyes and my mind filled with images of clouds. I could see the ocean very far below me — and then I saw canyons of sun-drenched white clouds. Suddenly I was happy and free, filled with an expansive joy I've never forgotten.

Was I seeing what the bird we had just buried was seeing? Was this that bird — come to life for a moment before departing for Heaven — or another bird?

When I reopened my eyes, the bird was gone.

Everything seemed absolutely still. Not a breeze. No more rain. Faintly I heard the ocean waves crashing at the bottom of the nearby cliffs.

Had I done it?

I was sure I had. With the force of my will and of my love, I had lifted the bird's spirit up and out of its earthly body. I had sent it on its path to a new life.

Was this what a witch could do?

I was the great-granddaughter and granddaughter of witches. Might I also be one myself? Then and there, at the age of six, I vowed that somehow, I would work on developing my natural talents and study the ways of witchcraft.

It was my family legacy.

Chapter Three

SUSSEX, ENGLAND, 1690

*F*ATHER'S TESTING OF OUR SPECIAL CLAIRVOYANT POWERS
went on for many years. By the time I was fifteen, it was
only me he tested. Kate had been excused nearly three years
earlier when her powers abandoned her, slowly becoming less
and less each day. Sometimes I suspected her of faking this
decline, though she swore to me that her lack of ability was real.

Truthfully, I hoped she was tricking Father because she hated
the long hours of testing. The idea that my abilities might also
disappear with age upset me deeply. Through the years I hadn't
lost my enthusiasm for learning witchcraft one bit, but the idea

had become more refined. I had no intention of wearing a black coned hat or cackling maniacally in the night. I certainly wasn't planning on acquiring warts of any kind.

I pictured myself in a cozy apartment in London, living independently, supporting myself on the money I earned from my special powers. I might read someone's mind to learn if he was cheating my client. Or I could possibly use my special sight to see into a locked safe to discern its contents. Maybe I would hear the thoughts of a man to learn if he really loved my client.

This picture of living without help from anyone thrilled me. Nothing else would do. I had to make it happen. The only way I could think of to set myself free from a humdrum domestic life — the only life a girl of my station could expect — was to continue developing my mental powers here in Father's study.

Besides, I couldn't abandon Father. I was his primary test subject. His work was well known among his colleagues, the other members of the Royal Society of London, a group of investigative scientists who were so well regarded that they advised kings and queens.

On this sunny spring afternoon, however, my mind was simply not engaged. Father appeared at the doorway of the cubicle where he'd stationed me within his large office. My chin was propped on my hands and I stared up at him, sighing forlornly because I had failed to *see* the drawings he was holding up in the other part of the laboratory. "I *am* trying, really," I insisted.

Father pushed back the long, black academic robe he wore over the flowing sleeves of his white shirt and dark pants. Returning my sigh with one of his own, he raked his hand over the thin remaining hairs of his balding head. "Maybe it's finally happened," he said unhappily.

"What has happened?"

Father lifted a pitcher containing water from a nearby table and poured it into a goblet. "Maybe not," he allowed, speaking more to himself than to me. "Perhaps you're only getting tired or thirsty."

"What do you think has finally happened?" I pressed. "Do you think I've lost the power?"

Father sighed again, studying my face.

"What?" I challenged. "What aren't you saying?"

"Let me explain to you as best I can. Earlier research has proven that most psychic ability is inherited and that in many cases, psychic ability diminishes with age; for most children it is all but gone by the time a child is five years old. My belief is that as verbal speech becomes firmly imbedded in a child's ability pool, telepathic power falls away, is suppressed. But in some cases, it is not."

"Do you mean, in cases such as mine?"

Father folded his arms thoughtfully. "Possibly."

"Do you think I am like a baby?" I asked a bit irritably. "That my mind is similar to that of a child?"

Here Father smiled and the expression on his face grew very tender. "I believe you are a pure and innocent girl with a beautiful mind, Elsabeth. I am always so proud of you. Psychic ability expresses itself most naturally in people with happy, outgoing natures such as yours."

Father's words made me smile, though I still worried that he meant I was childish. "What about Kate? Has she lost the power?"

"Yes, definitely. She lost the power completely by sixteen."

"Then I might too."

"Yes, you might."

I considered how I felt about this. Being able to see into the minds of those around me was the most natural thing in the world to me. I had been doing it for as long as I could remember. It had shocked me when I'd first learned that others *couldn't* do it.

"On the other hand," Father said, "there have been cases in which the power does not go away. In fact, it can also increase with age and practice."

"Is that what happened to my grandmother and my great-grandmother?" I knew it was a calculated risk to mention them. But I wanted to know.

Father nodded as the same faraway expression as always crept into his eyes.

"Tell me about both of them," I urged.

"You know about your great-grandmother?" Father questioned, looking very surprised.

"She advised Mary, Queen of Scots that she would be beheaded," I said, nodding. "Bronwyn told us years ago, when we were very young."

Father scowled at this and shook his head. "Bronwyn and your mother were so close they were like sisters. Otherwise I would have never kept her on as your governess."

"You wouldn't have?" I asked, surprised. "Why not?"

"Bronwyn and her entire clan can't let go of the old witchy ways of the backcountry. She's filled your and your sister's heads with her superstitions."

"Tell me about my grandmother and my great-grandmother."

"For centuries, our family has possessed psychic powers. It's an inherited ability. Some, like you, can see into the minds of others and can also envision what cannot actually be seen with the eyes, as with the pictures you can see even when they are not in front of you. Others in our family can predict the future." He looked at me as though trying to read something in my face. "It has produced both good fortune and terrible tragedy for us."

"Was your mother a witch?" I dared to ask.

"My mother was not a witch," Father insisted with feeling. "She was a midwife."

"She helped with the birth of babies?"

"Exactly. She was knowledgeable regarding herbal medicines and had surgical skills. But, in addition, she also had the family power."

"Is that why they thought she was a witch?" I asked.

Father nodded. "My mother could hear the thoughts of the unborn. It saved many little lives because she could hear when they were in distress."

"And that's why they killed her?" I thought of Bronwyn with her medicines and potions, and my skin prickled with fear for her. "Do such things still happen?"

"They do, I'm afraid. This is why I devote myself to testing for psychic ability — to prove it is not the work of the Devil but a legitimate ability. We live in a time of rational thought. Everything must be tested, measured, and quantified. I record how many pictures you see correctly, and I measure it over a long period of time and under varying conditions. I need to prove that psychic ability is a natural talent that can be cultivated rather than a thing mired in superstition and the suspicion of" — he circled with his hands as though searching for the right word — "mystical rites."

All at once it struck me. "You're afraid for Kate and me."

I stared him in the eyes and I saw clearly what image he harbored: Kate and me swinging from a hangman's noose. It was so horrifying that a startled gasp escaped my lips.

"What did you see?" Father demanded.

Opening my mouth to reply, I discovered my throat was too dry to speak. I kept seeing my own face, ashen and hollow-eyed, lips parched and cracked — my black tongue wedged in the right side of my mouth, protruding slightly. My head hung at an unnatural angle. My neck was broken.

I stumbled forward as the room spun.

Father caught me by my shoulders. "Elsabeth! What is it?!"

The room turned once more before I collapsed.

Chapter Four

J AWOKE A SHORT TIME LATER ON A COUCH IN FATHER'S laboratory. Father sat beside me, stroking my hand. "Are you all right, Elsabeth?" he asked.

Sitting up, I leaned on my elbows. My mind was strangely blank. I didn't want to recall what I had seen. "I saw something frightening that I read from your mind" was all I was able to tell him.

"But you can't recall it now?" Father pressed, his face filled with worry.

"No."

"I think you can but you don't want to."

"Maybe," I agreed reluctantly as the image of a figure dangling from the gallows returned to me, though this time it was a memory and not a vision.

"What you saw was in *my* mind. It is *not* the future," Father insisted. "It is only *my* fear." He sensed that I had seen something horrible and wanted to assure me. I wanted to believe that what he said was true.

"So I am able to mind read but not to see the future," I said, seeking clarification.

"Yes, I believe that is right."

Father took his powdered white wig from its stand and quickly fitted it over his balding head, tugging it into place. It was still quite crooked, so I stepped forward and adjusted its position. "What are you preparing for?" I asked.

"I'm expecting a guest," he replied with a final tug. There was a rap on the door of the laboratory, and Father looked sharply toward it. "I have a most exciting visitor today." He hurried to admit the knocking person.

"Greetings to you, sir," Father said with enthusiasm as a stocky man of middling height strode into the laboratory. He wore brown breeches and a brown robe over a flowing white shirt with a large ascot at his neck. Dark curly hair, which looked to be natural and not a wig, fell to his shoulders. He had a broad, round face, lively dark eyes, and high cheekbones. In his right hand he clutched a large, black, scuffed case.

"Allow me to present my daughter, Elsabeth James," Father said proudly. "Elsabeth, this is the great inventor and scientist Antonie Van Leeuwenhoek, come to visit us all the way from Delft."

Van Leeuwenhoek waved his left hand dismissively. "No need to be so grand, Sir Alexander. I am but a cloth merchant. I merely stumbled upon my discoveries in an effort to better see the cloth I deal with." His voice was gravelly and his Dutch-accented English was foreign to my ears.

"You are too humble," Father disagreed. "You are a man of indisputable brilliance, perhaps the greatest mind of our time."

Van Leeuwenhoek turned toward Father, beaming proudly. Laying his case on a table, he opened it and lifted one of the several smooth, round glass pieces inside. "This is my latest microscope lens. I've told no one about it yet. It magnifies up to five hundred times."

"Astounding!" Father cried.

Van Leeuwenhoek lifted a metal contraption that I recognized. I had seen a microscope in the science books Father had us read. "It's the invisible world of spit that I present on this day," he said, directing me toward the lens he'd placed on the microscope. He spit on a glass slide and set it under the microscope lens.

Peering down, my eyes widened in amazement at what I saw there. "What is that?!" I cried, backing away from the microscope.

"I call these tiny tiny creatures animalcules, my dear girl! Are they not marvelous?"

Marvelous wasn't the word I would have used. Although intriguing, they were also repulsive.

"Are those things alive?" I asked. "Are they actually animals?"

"They most certainly are!" Van Leeuwenhoek exulted. "They breathe, reproduce, and excrete. I also suspect that they communicate with each other."

I was stunned. And horrified!

Animals were living in my mouth?

"They are only one-celled organisms, you understand," Van Leeuwenhoek explained. "Infinitesimally tiny, but when magnified they are undeniably there."

"Are these one-celled things everywhere?" I asked.

"Everywhere!" Van Leeuwenhoek shouted. He studied me closely. "Ah, yes! You must be one of the psychically gifted, mind-reading daughters. I should have recalled that. Sir Alexander has told me all about your powers. How goes the work?"

"Encouraging," Father answered, though he scowled.

"You're not convincing me," Van Leeuwenhoek remarked.

At this, Father sighed. "There are so many within the Royal

Society who don't believe in psychic research as a real science. I encounter ridicule and skepticism at every turn."

"Hold steady, my friend," Van Leeuwenhoek advised. "Just as mine was scorned and then vindicated, so too shall your work be."

"Elsabeth," Father said, "would you please excuse me and Mr. Van Leeuwenhoek? We have business to conduct and need a bit of privacy."

"Certainly, Father," I agreed, dipping into a quick curtsy and heading out the door. What could they need privacy to talk about? I stood with my ear to the door, trying to hear, but their voices were too indistinct to make out. When I tried to focus in on Father's mind, his stream of thoughts ran too fast for me to follow.

I burned to know what they were saying.

Closing my eyes, I breathed deeply, trying to picture Van Leeuwenhoek, to recall his face as clearly as I could. Once I had a picture of him in my mind, I took a few deep breaths to help me clear my mind of its own eager thoughts and allow Van Leeuwenhoek's words to flood into my brain.

His thoughts came to me clearly. *She's the one I need. If anyone can help me with the animalcules, it is she.*

My fear and surprise shut down the mental communication. He was talking about me! How could I possibly help him with those eerie, tiny creatures?

✣

I thought about this all day and all night. The next day after my lessons, I changed into my swimming dress and headed out to the back lawn. After hours being cooped in Father's laboratory, to run in the fresh air was revitalizing. I pulled loose the blue satin ribbon binding my hair and let the salt air from the nearby ocean blow freely into it.

I reached the rocky bluff facing the ocean. Gazing down, I saw Bronwyn and Kate at the edge of the crashing ocean shore, the hems of their bathing dresses blowing as the white foam sprayed at their knees. It was no use shouting to them as I knew the surf would drown my voice, but they noticed me immediately and waved. Waving back, I began to navigate the rocky descent.

"So how was your afternoon in the stuffy old lab?" Kate asked tauntingly. "How did your witchy powers work today?"

"Not so well," I admitted.

"Pretend you don't have the powers, then. If you use them, everyone will say you're a witch. Even if they don't hang you for it, what man would want to marry you?"

"Elsabeth is not a witch," Bronwyn insisted. "Evil intent is required to be a witch. Psychic ability does not make her a witch."

"I'll be a witch if I want," I stated boldly, splashing Kate in the surf.

She laughed, dancing away from me. "Stop, Bethy!" she cried, kicking water back.

I grabbed at her ankle and pulled her leg out, sending her flying backward. As she toppled, Kate grabbed my wrist, dragging me into the ocean with her.

Laughing, we lifted ourselves, only to be taken down once more by the surprise of a crashing wave breaking on us from behind. I lost sight of Kate and the color-soaked world above as the white foam closed around me. Lying pinned by the ocean's force, I felt strangely content to let it hold me prisoner, knowing that in a moment it would release and allow me to rise again.

Hands appeared, groping in the foam. I was abruptly pulled into the sunshine, gasping and staring into Kate's laughing face. "You got a good dunking there," she observed brightly.

"Thanks for the hand," I replied, spraying her as I shook my wet hair.

Bronwyn rested a strong hand on Kate's arm. With her free hand, she held mine. "Girls, I must speak to you," she said in a serious tone. "When I heard that the great Van Leeuwenhoek was coming, I was filled with the strong intuition that some tremendous change would soon be upon us."

"Father will stop all this boring testing and start studying microscopes with Van Leeuwenhoek," I guessed with enthusiasm.

"I don't know, pet. You might be right," Bronwyn said.

"Do you really think so?" I asked, surprised at how her words alarmed me. I'd been joking, never really thinking Father would abandon his work.

"I don't know," Bronwyn admitted. "But last night while I was wondering what Van Leeuwenhoek's visit might mean to us, I decided to try an astral projection to see what I could discover."

At this I gasped, and my hands flew to my face in alarm. Since our girlhoods, Bronwyn had claimed to be able to rise out of her body and travel about the earth in something she called her astral body.

I well remembered the first time she told me of this power. I was seven and I had crept into her room one night, seeking her out to help me with a loose tooth.

Bronwyn was not in her bed but sat cross-legged on the floor, slumped against the wall, asleep. I couldn't even detect breath coming from her. Panicking, I began to shake her. When she wouldn't rouse, I was about to go for help, terrified that she was unconscious or worse. I was almost out the room when she called to me.

Tears of worry running down my cheeks, I threw my arms around her. "There, there, pet," she soothed, stroking my hair. "There's nothing to fear. Guess where I was."

"Where?" I asked, wiping my eyes.

"In India, at a most beautiful place called the Taj Mahal. Oh, I loved it. I wish you and Kate had been with me."

"In India?" I'd questioned, rubbing my eyes. "You're joking! How could you ever get to India and back in one night?"

That was when she told me that she would get into a state of meditation, and when she was in a deep-enough trance, her spirit would rise up from her body. I tried to imagine this and found it wasn't very hard to do. I had a book with drawings and it showed witches who flew across the moon at night.

"Do you ride on a broom?" I'd asked.

"Of course not!" Bronwyn had snapped with unusual ferocity. "Don't be ridiculous!"

"Sorry."

"I'm sorry too, pet. You just shouldn't say such things. It's dangerous."

"Why?" I asked, but she shushed the question away with a dismissive wave of her hand.

"Just put the thought out of your head," Bronwyn replied. "There's no broomstick involved."

"Can anyone leave their body to travel around?"

"That's a hard question. Do you know when you dream and then, in your dream, you feel that you've tripped on a step or on some stairs, or are even falling from a roof or a cliff?"

I had those dreams all the time, so I nodded.

"Well, some people, including me, believe that the falling dream is your astral body's first attempts to rise, but then — being inexperienced at it — falling back. To travel on the astral planes of existence, one must study and practice meditation so that the astral body keeps rising and does not fall."

"Can you teach me?" I asked hopefully.

"When you are grown, I will," Bronwyn said. "Astral travel is a serious art, not for children."

After that night, Bronwyn had never mentioned her astral travels to me again — at least not until this day. If I'd ventured a question, she'd simply put her finger to her lips and gently shush me. I was never quite sure if I believed her.

Kate's voice broke through this memory, returning me to the present moment. "Did you spy on Van Leeuwenhoek while you were in your astral body?" she asked Bronwyn.

"Late last night I went into his room while he slept," Bronwyn admitted. "On his desk, I found five vouchers for ocean passage. One of them was for a ship to carry him home to Holland."

"And the other four?" Kate inquired.

"The other four vouchers were for passage to America," Bronwyn revealed.

"America!" I gasped. She might as well have said they were tickets for a trip to the moon! I'd never even met anyone from America.

"Who do you think the tickets are for?" Kate asked.

Bronwyn pointed to Kate and me. "One, two . . ." She pointed to herself. "Three . . ."

"And Father is four," Kate concluded, to which Bronwyn nodded.

I couldn't even imagine what America would be like. Gazing out to the horizon of the ocean, I tried to picture a strange new world on the other side but nothing at all came into my head.

Maybe working with animalcules wouldn't be so terrible — if I could do it in America.

Chapter Five

*I*NSIDE OF A WEEK'S TIME, I FOUND MYSELF LOOKING BACK at dear England from the deck of a many-sailed ship, the *Golden Explorer*, headed for America. My respect for Bronwyn's powers had been vastly renewed. Van Leeuwenhoek had indeed changed our lives, just as she'd predicted. With incredible speed, Father rented the manor house to a family who wanted to spend the summer in the country. We were packed and out the door within a matter of days.

This idea of sailing abroad to study Van Leeuwenhoek's animalcules captivated Father's scientific imagination. The reminder of his grandmother and mother and of their tragic fate worried him, though. When he voiced his fears, Van Leeuwenhoek reassured him, "You will be working in isolation with my associate, using his laboratories in the city of Saint Augustine. I will join you there within the next month. These experiments will be conducted under conditions of utter secrecy. We don't want to open ourselves up to ridicule before we see if the work bears any fruit at all."

"Father, you know that I've never heard the thoughts of animals," I reminded him as we stood watching the churning waters below us. "I only see pictures in my head. I believe that might be how animals think, in images."

"So then you will tell us what images you see. When my mother worked with the unborn, they couldn't speak yet, but she sensed any discomfort or fear they might be expressing."

Bronwyn and Kate came alongside us. Kate was nearly green with seasickness and leaned heavily on Bronwyn. "Why don't you lie down in your bed below, Kate?" Father suggested.

Kate leaned forward over the side of the *Golden Explorer*. "That only makes things worse, Father," she replied. "It's stifling hot down there."

I felt so sorry for her. "How long will this voyage take?"

"Five to seven weeks depending on the weather conditions," Father reported.

Bronwyn put her arm around Kate's shoulders. "Come with me, pet," she soothed. "I have packed some ground ginger root, a remedy for nausea that will help you. Perhaps we can persuade the ship's cook to boil it in a tea for us."

"Bronwyn will fix her up," Father remarked as Kate and Bronwyn departed.

Many days were long and uninteresting. There were some children on board, younger than me, with whom I would play various games, just to pass the time. Their parents were content to let me occupy their offspring. I didn't mind since the children were pretty and lively.

In the evenings, we dined together at a long table next to the *Golden Explorer*'s kitchen. The quarters were tight, which forced everyone to be friendly. At every meal, Father sat beside and spoke to a man of learning named Reverend Finnias. They debated everything imaginable.

"The goal of natural history is to catalog the creations of the Lord," Reverend Finnias insisted one night.

"I disagree," Father replied. "This new age of scientific reason insists that we ask the question of how things work. We must be continually measuring and weighing our results in a scientific manner."

"Don't speak to me of science!" Reverend Finnias thundered. "Science is the portal by which the Devil works his malfeasance. Science makes people question God."

"Not at all," Father argued. "There is room in the world for both God and science."

These conversations stretched long into the nights. Though Father and Reverend Finnias could never seem to agree on anything, neither man ever lost interest in the debate.

After a few weeks of baking sun and mild breezes, the voyage was beset with stormy weather, day in and day out. It greatly impeded our progress. By the time we had been at sea for nearly seven weeks, we had not even reached the Bermudas. Although I was eager to be finished with this journey, I was nervous about reaching the island of Bermuda, which I had heard referred to as the Isle of Devils.

"Why is it called that?" I asked the helmsman, Felipe, one gray, rainy afternoon.

"It's a scary place, that's why," Felipe replied. "The waters are madly turbulent. Many ships go down by the Bermudas. I have heard reports of a giant, red-clawed hand that rises from the waves and pulls entire ships and their crews down to a watery grave."

I could picture the scene and it made me shiver. "Aren't you afraid to go there?" I asked.

Felipe shrugged. "Do not worry, my little friend. I have been watching the stars at night. We will pass through the deadly location in calm waters. All will be well."

I couldn't decide if he was telling me the truth or merely making up a tale to dispel my worry. "Are you sure?" I asked.

"Very sure."

Down in the lower deck, where Kate, Bronwyn, and I shared a very small space made up of a double-level bed and a cot with our cases clustered around to create a sort of room, Kate attempted to distract herself from constant seasick nausea by reading a volume containing the plays of William Shakespeare.

"How's the reading?" I asked her.

"Thank the heavens I have these plays or I would lose my mind," Kate replied.

Bronwyn came in, wrapped in her heavy blue robe, her hair braided. She peeked at Kate's open book and smiled. "Ah, you're reading the Scottish play, my favorite."

"*Macbeth*, yes," Kate confirmed. "Why is it your favorite?"

Bronwyn crawled under the covers of the narrow cot she slept in across from us. "Because it's Scottish and it has the three witches in it," Bronwyn replied. "They're really awful, frightening women, but they have all the best lines. Back in the fifteen hundreds, Scotland had terrible witch hunts. My mother told me about them. Her own mother was killed just as your grandmother was. Women were burned without any evidence against them at all."

"Why do you think Shakespeare made his witches so evil?" Kate questioned.

Bronwyn grunted, waving the question away. "Oh, he was playing up to King James the First, who was always ranting about witches. I think the king was just a sharp politician trying to scare his subjects so they'd worry about something other than the irresponsible way he was ruling them."

That night I had a nightmare where Kate, Bronwyn, and I were tied to a stake surrounded by straw. A man in a black executioner's mask was approaching us, a lit torch in his hand. Screaming with fear, I sat bolt upright, blessedly awake once more.

"Bethy, what's wrong?" Kate asked from below.

"Only a nightmare," I answered. "Sorry." After that, I couldn't fall asleep again. I was probably too frightened the dream might return.

Days and days passed, some stormy and others so calm that the ship could not seem to move forward at all. On one particular night, the sea was much calmer than usual, and though Kate remained belowdecks, there was color in her pale cheeks for almost the first time since we had departed England.

"Which play are you reading now?" I inquired as I perched at the foot of her bed.

"It's called *The Tempest*, Shakespeare's last play," Kate replied. "Shakespeare was inspired to write about a shipwreck on a deserted island because of the reports he was reading of shipwrecks off the coast of Bermuda and these other islands that we'll be coming to."

"Right where we are now?"

Kate nodded enthusiastically. "The English were only starting to explore the coastline at that time, and the sailors were sending back reports of terrible wrecks." Kate put the book down. "It's really a wild story about a wizard and his daughter who are shipwrecked on an island. It's full of magic and strange happenings."

"Do you think Shakespeare believed in magic?" I wondered.

"It certainly sounds like he does in *The Tempest*, but I don't know. It's only a story."

I returned to the upper deck, and immediately a warm breeze ruffled my hair. I saw Bronwyn looking out to sea. Her hair danced around her head, swept by the ocean breezes. The setting sun illuminated her face in a soft glow. "Beautiful night, pet, isn't it?" she commented when I joined her.

"Windy," I replied, holding my hair back so it wouldn't whip around my face.

"I love the wind. It's thrilling. One never knows what will blow in on a strong breeze." A powerful gust threw us both into the side of the ship. Bronwyn clutched my wrist to keep me from toppling completely. She laughed merrily, exhilarated, her blue eyes shining.

The wind flapped her skirts violently and she seemed to lift from the deck. A strong image flashed before me. I saw Bronwyn chuckling gleefully as she swooped and dipped, riding the air currents.

The picture was joyful yet unsettling. I closed my eyes to dispel it, and when I opened them once more, Bronwyn was in front of me, gazing into my eyes with concern. "Are you all right, Bethy? Did something frighten you?" she asked.

It felt foolish to ask her if she had just then been riding air currents, so I shook my head. "I'm all right."

Bronwyn put her arm around my shoulders and pulled me tight. "What an adventure we are having, eh, pet? What fun!"

I understood what she was feeling. I felt it too — that this trip would turn out to be the adventure of a lifetime.

Chapter Six

FELIPE HAD READ THE STARS INCORRECTLY. THE CONDITIONS near the Bermudas were very turbulent. And the rough weather continued for the next day and through the following night.

That night, I lay in the upper berth of the small sleeping compartment I shared with Kate and Bronwyn. The *Golden Explorer* pitched terribly in the howling wind and I could hear rain lashing the sails. Our only light was the short stub of a candle flickering in a glass lantern nailed to the wall. The candle threw long, wavering shadows against the wall and floor in an eerie display.

Below me, Kate moaned pathetically, one hand clutching her stomach while the other arm was flung across her forehead, in the grip of persistent nausea. How I pitied her! Bronwyn had soaked cold ginger tea in cloths and tied them around Kate's wrists. She had given her another cloth soaked in the ginger to inhale. I had no idea what further help I might be.

The *Golden Explorer* continuously dipped to one side and then rolled to the other. This relentless motion created a horrible queasiness in me, as well. If this was what Kate was experiencing without relief, I didn't know how she could bear it. Sometimes the tilt of the *Golden Explorer* was so extreme that I clutched the sides of my bed to keep from being tossed off. Pressing my head into the pillow, I fought the greasy stew I'd had for supper from coming up.

Strangely, Bronwyn was sleeping soundly on her cot, seemingly unaffected by the storm. "How *can* she sleep through this?" Kate complained to me, her voice thin and miserable.

"Maybe she isn't here," I suggested. "Perhaps she's left her body."

There in the wavering light, we both looked to Bronwyn, buried deep in the covers on her cot, noting her shallow breathing. Our governess was a sound sleeper, but she seemed especially lost to slumber's grip that night.

"I wish I could leave my body," Kate said. "I would give any-thing to be out of my body right now."

A deep wave of nausea swept through me and I had to wait for it to pass before I could reply. "So do I."

Shutting my eyes, I imagined Bronwyn's astral self flying back to the shore of Bermuda, the Isle of Devils. Was Felipe right? Did the Devil himself wreck ships; reach up to pull ships and their crews down into his own fiery home, as Felipe had told me? If Bronwyn was traveling out there tonight, would she encounter him?

Despite these alarming thoughts, and even with the awful rocking of the ship, I drifted into sleep. Within minutes, I was embroiled in a dream so real it was as if I were really there.

In the dream, I was walking through a pitch-dark forest, drenched in a storm. Wind-tossed trees bent nearly to the ground. Lightning scribbled jagged lines of brilliance across the rain-soaked sky. I was searching for Bronwyn, calling her name over and over even though my voice was being carried off by the wind.

Finally, I saw a fire and followed its flickering light until I came to an open hut. Inside it, Bronwyn sat with three other women around the fire. A branch snapped under my foot, drawing the attention of the women. Bronwyn's face was cold when she saw me. A menacing light emanated from her usually warm eyes. She beckoned me to come closer, but something within me wouldn't allow me to take a step in her direction. Then I real-ized what was frightening me. By Bronwyn's side stood a huge black dog. Its eyes glowed yellow and its fangs were bared. It snarled at me.

My eyes snapped open as the *Golden Explorer* dipped severely to the right. An almost deafening boom came from above, and then a thud as something of immense weight hit the deck overhead, rattling the walls of our cabin. "Kate!" I cried. "What was that?"

"I'm here!" Kate called from across the room. She stood bent over Bronwyn. "I was scared and tried to wake her, but she won't stir."

Scrambling from my berth as quickly as I could manage, I groped my way over toward the two of them.

"I'm shaking her, but she won't respond," Kate said, a sob of fear in her voice.

I leaned over Bronwyn's face. At first I could detect no breath, but in the next moment I realized she was emitting slow, shallow puffs of air.

"We should get Father," Kate said, and then fell back against the wall as the *Golden Explorer* rolled once more. Clutching her mouth to fight down the seasickness, she lost the battle and vomited.

My nausea had subsided, so I volunteered to go get Father. As soon as I left our cabin, I saw him in his nightshirt, hurrying toward me, holding a lit lantern. "Get your sister and Bronwyn and come above," he said.

Shouting above the din of the storm, I informed him franti-cally that we couldn't rouse Bronwyn. He dashed past me into our cabin. "Bronwyn, wake up!" he bellowed, shaking her roughly by her shoulder. "Get up!"

When she still did not wake, Father handed Kate the lantern and scooped Bronwyn into his arms. "Put on your capes and bring blankets, girls, and that's all," he commanded. "Get a blan-ket for Bronwyn."

I scurried about the cabin, rapidly collecting those things. In minutes, Kate and I were wrapped in both our capes and blan-kets. I stepped into my high boots but didn't take the time to buckle them.

"Hurry!" Father commanded us, braced against the doorjamb to steady himself, the slumbering Bronwyn still in his arms. Within seconds, Kate and I were hurrying ahead of him on the narrow ladder to the deck. The moment my head came above the hatch, I was doused with rain as though someone had hurled a thousand buckets of it at me. Pulling myself up, I immediately slipped on the soaked deck and slid until I hit the port-side rail.

Crew members ran in all directions. Some were above, clutch-ing the rigging, battered by the gale as they attempted to lower the flapping sails. Four crew members struggled to toss a rowboat over the side. Other passengers appeared, looking bewildered and terrified.

A sail ripped from its mast and beat against the other sails, drumming with deafening noise. A jagged line of lightning sizzled along the rigging lines that held the sails, and an earsplitting blast of thunder immediately followed. It took only minutes for the sails to burst into flame, throwing sparks down to the deck below.

Father put his hand on my arm. Bronwyn was now slung over his shoulder like a sack, and Kate was at his side. "Get to the boats! This way," he shouted through the driving rain, above the wind's tumult.

A flaming shard of broken wood pierced the deck between us as though someone had aimed a fiery arrow from above. Before the rain could douse it, the trim of Kate's cape caught fire. Father stomped it with his boot as Kate screamed.

When it was out, we ran alongside Father to the bow of the boat. Fishing nets had been rolled over the side, dropping down to the turbulent ocean below.

Peering over the edge, I saw crew members in three violently rocking rowboats that had been tossed into the water from the ship. Surely there was not room for everyone on board to fit into them.

Men and women were climbing past me over the ship's side, some of them clutching small children, the bigger children climbing on their own. They were the ones I had played with earlier in the voyage. Terror now twisted their faces.

Still slung on Father's shoulders, Bronwyn suddenly opened her eyes and leapt from his arms, tottering for a moment beside him. She was completely alert, assessing the situation. "Girls! Over the side! Quickly! Quickly!" she insisted, as though she had been conscious all along.

Kate's eyes were full of panic, and I knew how she felt. The idea of climbing the nets while being pounded by fierce rain was awful enough. But the *Golden Explorer* was rocking at an ever more severe pitch from side to side. With a thunderous crack, one of the flaming masts crashed to the deck. Instantly, a line of flames raced toward us.

Kate and I scrambled to avoid the attacking fire. Not even the driving rain was sufficient to quell the flames. Father and Bronwyn were quickly beside us, directing us toward the nets. "You can do it, girls. Climb down!" Father said with surprising calm.

Lifting me by the waist, Father swiftly swung me overboard, holding on until I could grip the top netting. Taking courage from his composure, I began to climb down. My hands and feet slid and the soaked ropes burned my skin. The rain was so blinding that I was only dimly aware of Kate's form on the netting some feet away from me. With a howl, a gust of wind tore away the blanket I had wrapped around my shoulders. It sailed through the black sky, a giant sea bird flapping, until it disappeared.

I heard a shout and thought it was Kate calling to me.

Instinctively, I stretched out my hand to the blurred shape I took to be my sister. My fingers clutched only air. And then I could no longer even see her form.

A body plummeted past me, only inches away. Looking down, I saw the person splash into the waves below. A rowboat moved toward the spray and I assumed it was attempting a rescue.

I gripped the net, paralyzed with fear. "Kate!" I shouted. "Bronwyn! Father!"

The wind snapped the words from my mouth, racing them out to sea.

I concentrated on nothing but placing my hands methodically one below the other. Rung by rung my foot searched for the net's lower roping until it found a foothold.

With a shrill creak, the ship's hull leaned out over me.

The netting hung at a ninety-degree angle away from the *Golden Explorer*.

My feet slid off the ropes and dangled in air.

I clutched fiercely to the netting, ignoring the burn from the rope. Screams and shouts hit my ears even over the howling wind.

Then a new, even more terrifying reality came to me: The *Golden Explorer* was not rocking back in the direction from which it had come! It would have already been moving in the opposite direction, if it were going to go.

No, it had reached its tipping-over point and was heading steadily downward. If it kept going, it would crash right on top of the rowboats below.

The *Golden Explorer*, with its flaming sails, was capsizing.

It would plunge all of us who clung to the nets into the dark, cold, rain-lashed sea. We would be underwater with the gigantic ship pinning us below.

Down in the smaller boats, the crew was rowing madly out of the way. People fell from the nets on every side of me. I winced and cringed each time the flapping, wind-tossed rope flung another screaming person into the black ocean.

The *Golden Explorer*'s hull menaced us with ominous creaks as it continued its slow descent into the sea.

My terror was almost too much to stand. Where was my sister? Bronwyn? Father? Were they already floundering in the water below?

My hand slid and I lost hold of the net.

Suddenly I was in the air, attached to nothing.

My cape ballooned out, and an intense silence enveloped me as I hung like a hawk, riding an air current.

Then I pitched headfirst and tumbled through the air.

Chapter Seven

J HIT THE OCEAN WITH MY CAPE WRAPPED AROUND MY head. The heavy woolen material was instantly soaked and pulled me down like a weight. Seizing its ties, I ripped the cape off.

The instant the heavy cloth fell away, I was in a yellow world, and I swirled below the ocean's surface in a vortex of seawater. Looking up, it seemed that the sun had fallen to earth and its fire was engulfing everything.

People flailed all around me. Others only hung there, feet and legs waving listlessly.

A bubble of air dribbled from my lips and I clamped down on it. I was deep underwater with only a mouthful of air!

Snapping my legs together, I stroked forcefully toward the flaming surface.

Where was my family?

I didn't see any of them. But I couldn't look for long. With only minutes left, nothing could be allowed to distract me.

As I rose, my lungs churned with pain. It took all my self-control not to inhale the salty sea. My chest was exploding. The blinding light on the surface grew brighter still.

Almost there . . .

A cascade of bubbles shot from my mouth. Gasping and coughing, I broke through the water and inhaled deeply. The air seared my throat. Had I sucked in flame? I expelled it with hard force. Leaving only a cheek full of roasted air, I ducked below once more.

The salt sea burned my scorched skin but it also cooled.

The *Golden Explorer*'s massive hull had become an inferno. The bowed wall of flaming wood lay on its side. Its metamorphosis from majestic vessel to underwater shipwreck was now inevitable.

With a thunderous creak and bang, the ship continued tipping. The movement set off a watery surge that pushed me below the surface even farther.

I had to get away from the sinking ship. And I needed to find another place to come up for air. If the *Golden Explorer* sank completely, all of us would be trapped in the masts and sails. We'd surely drown.

Turning, I began to swim away from the boat, but my air was going fast. I headed back toward the top of the water, swimming at a diagonal. This time, when I broke the surface, a wave knocked me back and filled my open mouth with salt water and rain. I spat it back out and inhaled deeply. The rain and waves made it impossible to see anything clearly other than the flaming ship.

It seemed safest not to swim too far because I still hoped one of the rowboats might pick me up. Also, I needed to find Kate, Bronwyn, and Father. I hovered there in the water, far enough from the burning ship but not so far as to be on my own.

Debris from the belongings of passengers and crew members and from the wreckage of the *Golden Explorer* floated on the waves. I thought I saw Father's book of Shakespeare plays float by and grabbed for it but couldn't connect. It certainly made no difference. The book was nearly destroyed.

A large wave swelled toward me, and on its crest was an open barrel turned on its side. The wave tossed the barrel into the air as it curled over me. Fearing that I would be crushed by its force, or hit by the flying barrel, I dove below. When I emerged, the barrel floated nearby.

Swimming to it, I pulled myself inside.

Off a short distance, I could see the *Golden Explorer*. Reaching out, I paddled, but a wave rolled up below the barrel, lifting it and launching it through the air. Gripping the sides with my hands, I braced with my legs as I flew through the dark storm. The barrel splashed back into the ocean, dipped, and took on water, but thankfully didn't sink.

Waves splashed inside, hitting me with salt water over and over. Shivering, I gripped and braced again as once more the barrel was lifted and thrown through the storm-tossed night.

This terrible ride went on and on without end. My teeth rattled each time the barrel landed, only to be swept up on a fresh wave and pitched into the air. Yet I didn't dare to leave the flying container. To be out in the water would be much worse.

The barrel floated peacefully for a few moments, allowing me to loosen my grip on its sides. How my muscles ached! As it bobbed on the tempestuous waters, I thought I saw a hazy full moon appear in the sky. Was the storm abating? The rain seemed less fierce.

From a long way away, white fingers of foam began to roll toward me, picking up strength and height. I watched the wave's ominous approach with dread. The tide was coming and there was nothing I could do about it.

Would it be better to leave the barrel, to avoid this rapidly growing wave by diving under? If I did that, I would lose my little craft for certain and then where would I be? Adrift in the open ocean, where I would surely tire and sink? And who knew what creatures swam here?

Resolving to stay, I gripped the sides of the barrel with all my strength and once more braced my legs across the width of the barrel.

The wave was becoming so gigantic that I couldn't stand to look at it for fear that I would pass out from utter terror. The last thing I saw before squeezing my eyes shut was a wall of water coming at me.

The barrel sped along this giant wall at a high speed. Never before had I ever traveled at such a velocity. My heart raced, slamming into my chest.

I had to open my eyes, needed to see what was happening.

The huge wave shot me from its tunnel. Screaming, I held on for my very life as the wave flipped the barrel onto the top of its mighty arch.

The barrel bounced on the crest for what seemed a very long moment before being tossed so high I felt as if I was being rocketed toward that hazy moon in the sky.

Someone was pounding on my head, and it was making me angry. Opening my eyes, I didn't know where I was for a moment.

In the next second, though, everything that had happened came to me in a rush of memory.

Blinking hard, I gazed into blinding sunshine. The barrel had flipped up so that its bottom bobbed in the ocean and the sun's rays beat down on me. I sat with my knees to my chin in warm rainwater, my hair dripping and my white nightgown plastered to my skin.

No one was pounding on my head. The hammering was *in* my head.

The spot that hurt the most was above my right eye. I touched it and winced as excruciating pain raced across my forehead. My hand came back smeared in red. Curious, I poked the spot and recoiled in agony. Cautiously, not wanting to tip the barrel and be spilled, once more, into the sea, I rose to take in my surroundings.

I was alone, in a barrel, bobbing in a vastness of sky and ocean, with no sign whatsoever that the *Golden Explorer*, its passengers, or crew had ever been there.

Chapter Eight

$\mathcal{B}$Y SHIFTING MY WEIGHT FORWARD AND BACK SEVERAL times, I was able to rock the barrel back onto its side. After that I could lie down and let the waves push me along on their rolling surf. When seaweed drifted by, I grabbed it, devouring the slippery green leaves as though they were a great treat.

Despite the rounded hardness of my bed, I easily fell asleep in the evenings as the sun set, lulled as peacefully as a baby in a rocking cradle.

On the first night, I dreamt of Bronwyn flying through a sky of deep blue dotted by purple clouds. I climbed onto the outside of my barrel and called to her, waving my arms. She swooped down and sat beside me.

I was overjoyed and hugged her, squeezing hard.

"There's my brave girl," Bronwyn soothed, stroking my hair. "How thankful I am that I taught you to swim."

"Have you seen Kate? Father?" I asked.

"Not yet. You're the first I've found. Are you frightened, pet?"

"Terribly frightened," I admitted.

"Hmmm, you must be," Bronwyn said, rubbing my back. "Here's a song that my mother taught me when I was little. It's got a bright tune. It's called 'The Water Is Wide.'"

"That's surely true," I said, sweeping my arms out over the expanse of ocean. "It's wide as wide can be."

"Exactly." Bronwyn tossed back her snowy hair and lifted her face to the moon as she sang in the low, lovely, melodic voice I'd heard so often.

> The water is wide, I can-not cross o'er.
> And neither have I the wings to fly.
> Build me a boat that can carry two,
> And both shall row, my true love and I.
>
> A ship there is and she sails the seas.
> She's laden deep, as deep can be;

But not so deep as the love I'm in
And I know not if I sink or swim.

Bronwyn sang it again, and this time I joined her, both of us singing loudly. For the time, it was as though nothing at all was wrong. It was just Bronwyn and me sailing the open sea on a barrel, off on a great adventure.

"Did you ever have a true love, Bronwyn?" I asked.

Her face grew soft with memory. "Indeed I did. It was a long time ago, but I can see him still."

"What happened?"

"We married."

"You were married, Bronwyn? Why have you never told us?"

"He was conscripted to go fight the Spanish under the rule of Oliver Cromwell. He was killed. I never wanted another. He was the greatest love of my life. When I think of him, I try to be happy for the time we spent together."

"I wonder if I'll ever have a great love?"

"Ah, you will, Bethy. I have no doubt. You have a great heart, and it will draw great love to it."

I wasn't as sure, but I hoped she was right.

We sat quietly side by side as the barrel was pushed by the waves. After a while, an awful idea struck cold chills down my spine. "Bronwyn, are you . . . alive and traveling . . . or are you . . . are you . . ."

"Dead?" Bronwyn supplied the word I couldn't bring myself to utter. "To tell you the truth, pet, I'm not quite sure myself. I was traveling when the storm hit, which was why you couldn't wake me at first. Then when I returned to my body and fell from the netting, I struck my head hard on the side of a rowboat. In the next instant I was traveling again."

"Could you see your own body below?" I asked.

"No. I wonder if it fell into the water or if someone pulled me into the boat. If I find my way back to my body, I don't know if I will be dead or alive."

"Are you frightened?" I asked.

"Not yet," Bronwyn answered serenely. "I have been busy so far looking for you, Kate, and your father. I will find my body. The astral self has the ability to do so, much like certain birds can always find their way home."

"And what if you're not alive?" I dared to ask.

"I don't know yet, pet. I haven't figured it out. Perhaps I'm not dead or alive." A faraway expression came to her face, which struck me as very beautiful there, illuminated by the moon. "Maybe I'm a ghost, or perhaps I'm only a dream."

"A dream?!" I cried, alarmed. "No, not a dream!"

My eyes snapped open and I was once more inside my barrel. A huge full moon threw a line of silver along the ocean and shone directly on me. The distant lines of surf dazzled with their rolling light.

Sitting up, I searched the sky for my beloved governess. "Bronwyn," I murmured aloud. I had felt comfort from her presence.

A dream? Or perhaps it had been real. I couldn't tell.

Chapter Nine

*I*N THE NEXT DAYS I SANG "THE WATER IS WIDE" OVER AND over just to keep my mind occupied, and it did brighten my mood a bit and distract me from my hunger and thirst. I napped a great deal and kept a look out for more seaweed, though none came. I tried to keep track of day and night and how long I floated, but my hunger, exhaustion, and thirst made my mind hazy and I lost count.

One night, I dreamt of Van Leeuwenhoek. He and I were gazing through a microscope down at a dish of his animalcules. I realized that I could hear them chattering. Leaning down close,

I could make out sentences: "Don't say that. God is always listening. God will hear."

I awoke, distressed by such an odd dream. Had the animalcules mistaken me for God? Was I the one they worried was listening?

Watching the moonlit sea a while longer, I fell back to sleep and dreamt again.

This time I dreamt that I rolled over in my barrel and opened my eyes. Bronwyn was staring in at me. She reached her hand out and I took it. Instantly, I was up in the sky with her, flying across the full moon. It was a rousing romp over waves and ocean.

"Are you a witch, Bronwyn?" I asked her.

"I mean no evil, so I am not a witch," she replied. "Power is not witchcraft."

The next day, when I opened my eyes, I felt refreshed and happy from the dream. As I came fully awake, I realized that there was a new sound outside the barrel. It was no longer the monotonous roll and crash of distant waves. This was the splash of pounding surf.

Sitting up, I peered out and took in the wondrous sight of a glistening sand beach. Behind it was a forest of ferns and tropical-looking foliage. The water here sparkled with bluer hues than out in the dark ocean.

Sliding from the barrel, I tried to swim hand over hand but discovered that I was too weak. Instead, I lay on my back, stroking as best I could and letting the current carry me forward.

Near the shore, the surf crashed, throwing white spray into the air and rolling me off my back. As I came to my feet, I let the breakers push and knock me under without caring; I was so filled with elation at seeing solid ground.

When I finally emerged from the pounding surf and staggered forward, my legs buckled beneath me, dropping me to my knees.

I knelt in the shallows of the surf between ocean and land. A warm breeze wafted around me as I absorbed the reality of my new situation.

I was alive and I was on land!

But I was alone and scared. What would happen to me?

Where was Kate? Father? Were they even alive?

Had I really seen Bronwyn? Had she been just a dream?

And then the odd, floaty, mental limbo I was in broke. Everything became vivid. I was in a world of bright color and sound: Waves crashed, birds squawked, the leaves whispered in the ocean breeze. I was famished, weak, exhausted. My muscles ached, my throat was sore, my lips were cracked.

Unbridled tears flooded from my eyes. All the fears I couldn't afford to think about those days in my lonely, wet barrel overpowered me now. Loud, racked shouts of despair emanated from deep within me.

I knelt there in the surf of this strange land, engulfed in my own vast sorrow.

I don't remember crawling up onto the beach, or even falling asleep, but I must have done so, because I awoke encrusted in sand, with my back against a boulder.

The gentle lavender-gray of pre-dawn revealed a calm ocean pulsing against a sublime beach dotted with large pieces of gnarled, sundried wood. Despite the earliness of the hour, the heat was already tangible, as though it was a blanket wrapping itself around my body.

In this paradise I felt myself to be a sand-coated barnacle, a seabird with broken bones tossed on the shore, a crab with a cracked shell. It was as if sand had found its way into my very joints. My physical complaints were too numerous to count — jagged fingernails, blistered lips, splinters, and cuts, to name only a few.

The most awful hurt by far was the roar in my belly. The twist and churn of my stomach was like no pain I'd ever endured. Its agony reached into my brain, filling me with a furious rage at one moment and deathlike despair at the next. Yet I didn't have the strength required to get up and search for food. I didn't even have the stamina to sit up from my prone position.

Though the weather was hot, my teeth chattered. And that's when — through the blur of my rising tears — I saw the miracle.

A mere arm's reach from me was a green basket woven from some sort of reed. The shinier, more vivid green showing on top seemed to be a lining made from some sort of big leaf. Reaching as quickly as my aching arms could manage, I pulled the woven basket toward me. Inside was a hand-carved wooden bowl filled to the top with brown rice.

Was this a dream? If it was, I didn't care.

With trembling hands, I shoveled the sticky grains into my mouth, barely chewing or tasting, only consuming. In a few more minutes, the nutty goodness spread through my body, wrapping me in bliss. Never had any other food given me such complete pleasure.

But who had left this bowl of rice?

Of course I hoped that the rice meant that there were people nearby who could help me. Why had they not shown themselves?

The only thing to do was to set out in search of these people. To keep cool, I walked at the edges of the water — splashing through, the ocean breeze whipping my nightgown, tossing my hair. My muscles still ached, but the rice and the beauty of my surroundings had gone far to revive my body and spirit.

My travels took me along marshland bordered by tall grass. Birds called back and forth to one another, and insects buzzed and chirped in a nonstop cacophony. I jumped back, startled, when a pair of whitish-blue wings with the same expanse as my own outspread arms rose up from out of the grass.

An angel? It was a fantastical thought, but it was the first thing that came to my mind.

The next moment revealed the creature to be a most beautiful bird with a long graceful neck and elongated legs. I'd seen it in a book once — a blue heron. The bird landed in the marsh waters, dipping its neck to fish for its supper. Rising again, with a smallish fish in its beak, it once more spread its majestic wings and flew away.

It wasn't all perfection, though. I began swatting high-whining mosquitoes as I walked. I also cut my heel, just a little, on a sharp stick.

The marsh seemed to end at the foot of a shadowy wooded area. Immense, wide-spreading oaks with thick branches emanating from a single thick trunk grew close together. Each oak was draped in fat strands of Spanish moss that fell straight down from its branches. The giant trees were so tightly packed that I had the impression that I would be entering an interior rather than an outdoor space if I were to step under the canopy of their leaves.

I considered exploring this area, but feared going in where there might be unfamiliar wildlife and where hazards would be less easily seen. After I knew my way around a little better, I would venture into the tangled forest.

Heading back the same way I had come, I followed the marshland and then the shoreline back to the spot at which I'd begun. I could recognize the place easily because I'd left the woven basket atop the boulder beside which I'd slept..

By the time I got back to the boulder, the sun was well past its highest point — I guessed it to be between three and four o'clock. I was once again famished . . . and very thirsty.

And I also had the strongest sensation that someone was watching me.

Mus tek cyear a de root fa heal de tree.

The voice was inside my head and I heard it clearly.

Father had taught us Spanish, French, and some Latin. I recognized a few English words in the sentence but I had no idea what it meant.

"Hello?" I called, aiming my voice toward the boulder where I most strongly sensed the presence. "Are you there? Can you help me?"

No one answered, and a nervous fear slowly crept through me. What if this person wasn't friendly? It might not be the same individual who had left the rice earlier.

Udat tittuh? Ibidio?

I heard the voice again in my head. This time I could tell it was a male voice. From the inflection, I realized he was asking a question. Was he wondering who I was and why I was there?

I waved my arm widely. "Hello! Can you help me?"

Njoso?

What sort of language was this? Where exactly was I? Could I have blown so far off course that I was in China, or Egypt, or Africa? I hadn't been at sea more than three days. Was it possible?

Anxious but eager to discover who this could be, I began walking toward the boulder. Almost at once there was a rustling in a bush behind it. "Don't go!" I shouted. "Please don't go! I won't hurt you!"

A branch snapped farther off. The person was leaving. I broke into a run, desperate to catch whoever it was. Beyond the boulder was thick foliage that I tore through, leaping over tangled vines and fallen trees. I stopped, though, when I came to more of the moss-strewn trees. Again, I was not willing to enter that realm of dim, dappled half-light.

My mind was on this strange encounter as I returned to my boulder. As soon as I got there, I checked the basket to see if my visitor had left me anything new. There was more rice, and this time it was dotted with some kind of vegetable I'd never seen before — a green oblong cone about as long as my fingers. It was warm, as was the rice.

Somewhere nearby, someone was cooking.

Beside the bowl was a metal container loosely covered with another piece of metal. When I opened it, I cried out with pleasure.

Three pieces of hot coal glowed at the bottom of the can.

Forgetting my food for the moment, I raced out onto the beach with my container of coals. Setting it down with the utmost care, I pulled together a pile of the bleached-white branches that were all over the beach and carried them back to the boulder. There I built them into a tower and tipped the burning coals on top. I smiled broadly as it burst into flame.

After a hot supper, I searched the beach for every piece of wood I could find so that my wonderful conflagration wouldn't die down. Luckily, deadwood was plentiful on the beach.

That night, I lay beside my fire, listening to the thundering waves. A crescent was missing from the side of the waning full moon, but it still threw silver ribbons on the restless sea.

Something black flew across the moon and I guessed it was a bat. It made me think of Bronwyn. Was she still flying around out there or had she found her way back to her body? I thought she must be back in her body — otherwise why didn't she come to find me as she had on those other nights out at sea? And then I recalled that she might not have really come at all. Those late-night visits might have been — probably were — a dream. Still, I hoped they'd been real.

Sitting back on my elbows, I gazed up at the expanse of stars twinkling against the velvety deep blue night. What was out there? The mysteries of the world seemed so vast and unknowable.

A brilliant light twinkled across the night. A shooting star! I made a wish — *Let Father, Kate, and Bronwyn be safe!*

The steadily pounding surf lulled me and I curled up on the sand, my knees pulled to my chest, my hands tucked under my head for a pillow.

I wondered what would happen to me. It was no good for me to just stay here on the beach.

Tomorrow I would not let the mysterious trees frighten me, I decided. When the sun came up, I would enter the forest and try to discover who else was living here.

Chapter Ten

*I*N THE MORNING, MY RUMBLING STOMACH DEMANDED FOOD and water. I glanced to the boulder, hoping to spy another gift from my mysterious benefactor, but there was nothing.

Heading into the surf, I wondered where to begin digging for oysters or clams. Was there a sign to look for? As I pondered this, I wandered knee-deep into the water, wiggling my toes in the sand, hoping to detect the hard shell of an oyster.

"No! No!"

It was the male voice I'd heard the other day. But this voice was *not* in my head.

A young man with very dark skin and very dark hair was running toward me, waving his arms wildly. He wore a blue cotton shirt that was half open and blew behind him. His tan pants were held up with a green reed and his feet were bare. Around his neck he wore a blue glass bead tied to a leather cord. He was about my age, maybe a little older.

"Get out of there!" he shouted as he splashed through the surf. With amazing speed, he scooped me into his arms and ran back onto the beach, where he gently put me down. "There are sharks in those waters!" he cried. "They feed right in this area."

Never in my life had I seen a person with such black skin. In a London Museum, I had once seen a statue carved of ebony; this young man's skin was just as black and I thought him every bit as beautiful as the statue. I was so enchanted at the sight of him that words failed to form in my mind or mouth.

"Sharks!" he exclaimed, exasperated by my blankness. "You know what they are, don't you?"

I didn't, so I shook my head.

He held his arms wide and I could see he was strong, with lean muscles. "It's a big, big fish with *very* sharp teeth." The picture that formed in my head was nothing I had ever seen — it was coming directly from his mind. And it was awful — a man lying on the beach, blood spilling from his hip from where his leg used to be but was no more.

I gasped sharply in horror, my hands flying to my face.

"Yes!" he shouted, seeing that I suddenly comprehended. "It will eat you. It's very horrible. Believe me. I have seen what a shark can do."

I knew that was true.

He gestured toward the ocean. "They come in very close this time of year. No one on the island swims here. Bin yah don't swim at all, really. Only the comeya get eaten."

"Bin yah? Comeya?" I questioned, confused.

He smiled. "That's island Gullah," he explained. "Bin yah are from families who have been on the island for twenty years, since the first plantations were settled here. The comeya are newcomers, folks who have not been here nearly as long, like me." His voice was low and he had an accent that I didn't recognize.

"You speak English. Where am I?" I asked.

"Of course I speak English. Back in Africa — before I came here — I worked for the Richards and George Company. They export palm oil from Africa. My father and I were employed by them since I was a buhbuh."

"A what?"

"A little boy."

"I speak English and I have never heard the word *buhbuh*," I said. "Is it more Gullah?"

"Yes."

"What is Gullah?"

"It's what we speak here. Some words are English; others are from my home in Africa, Sierra Leone, and other nearby places and tribes."

"Are we in Africa?" I asked.

He roared with laughter. "You are a crazy girl! No, you are in America. How is it that you don't know where you are? Are you lost?"

"I'm very, *very* lost," I told him. "The ship I was on sank. I floated here in a barrel."

"A barrel?!" he cried incredulously. "What a brave girl you are! A barrel?!"

"I was lucky to find it. I wouldn't have survived if I hadn't."

The young man rubbed his chin. "I thought you were a njoso — a forest spirit."

That made *me* laugh. "You did?"

"Yes. I left you gifts so you would be good to the people of my village."

"I thank you very much for them, even though I am not a forest spirit. They kept me alive."

"How can I be sure you are not a forest spirit?" he asked, though I sensed that now he was teasing. "It is the only explanation. You are obviously not Gullah — you are far too pale for that. And in that raggy dress, I can tell you are not ibidio either."

The words *njoso* and *ibidio*: I'd heard them the other day. Now that he spoke, I realized he was the one who had been watching me. "What do you mean by those?" I asked. "More Gullah?"

He nodded. "Ibidio is the white man, the slave owners. If you were of a slave-owner family, you would be dressed much finer than that."

"Slave owners?" I questioned. "Are you a slave?"

A slave. What a horrible thing. I didn't want to sound as upset as I felt.

"Born free in Sierra Leone, but when my father was captured and enslaved, I was with him. When he died last year, I was shipped here from Bunce Island. I'm being trained to be a driver, which I don't really like, but there are worse things."

"What do you drive?"

"People."

"People?"

"Most of the bosses are gone now for the summer. They won't be back until the fall. It's too hot for them now. Plus, they don't want the yellow fever and malaria. It doesn't affect us like it does them. In fact, we brought the diseases with us from West Africa."

"You did?"

"They call West Africa 'The White Man's Grave.' The slavers are afraid to even come ashore."

"They should have stayed away," I remarked.

"Oh, how I wish that they had," he agreed. "Well, we brought lots of things from home with us, and those illnesses were among them." He shrugged. "We did not ask to come."

"So the slave keepers are not here now?"

"No. They take off and leave us on our own when it gets too hot for them to bear. Things are much, much nicer here when they're gone. You picked a good time to come. This is the happy time of year."

"I didn't exactly select it," I pointed out.

"True, but you're in luck, just the same. It's very hot, though. I have to admit that."

"You said you are a driver. Where do you drive the people?"

At this, he laughed heartily. "I drive them crazy!"

"What do you mean?" I asked, not understanding but smiling, because his laughter was contagious.

"I *drive* them onward to keep working. A driver is a slave foreman. It's the slave guy who is in charge when the white bosses are gone."

"Have they taught you about rice farming?"

"No, funny girl, *we* teach *them*. On the West Africa coast, we grow rice, so the slavers in this part of America ask for us in particular because we know more about rice farming than they do. Before he was enslaved, my father was a rice farmer and he taught me." His expression became distant. I felt certain he was remembering his childhood in Sierra Leone, and didn't want to listen in to be sure.

"They picked me to be a foreman because the tea company trained me as a stock boy and taught me to read and write English so I could do the job. As well as my native Fula, I can also speak both Gullah and English. People think we only use Gullah here on the island, but I learned it back on Bunce Island. It's a language that blends English with African words from many different African tribes. It helped to have one way to communicate when so many captives were coming into the Bunce Island port from such varied areas, speaking so many different languages. Mostly the words are from West Africa."

"Where are we?"

"Wadmalaw Island. By the way, I am named Aakif," he said, taking my hand. "The bosses call me John, but I don't use that name among my family and friends. What can I call you — since we are going to be friends?"

His words made me smile. Somehow I knew he was right; we would be friends. There was nothing psychic about it. The feeling came from the warmth of his smile, the fact that in some strange way — although we'd just now met — he seemed happy to see me. I felt oddly pleased to see him too, as though somehow we'd always known each other and we were reuniting rather than meeting for the first time.

"Then I should call you Aakif," I said.

"Of course. And what should I call you?"

"Elsabeth."

He shook his head thoughtfully. "Too long."

"Bethy?" I suggested.

He considered this. "Betty-Fatu."

"But that's also long," I pointed out. "And why that?"

"Fatu is African and it's a name I like. It's easier to say than Elsabeth."

Again, I found myself smiling broadly. "I like it also. Betty-Fatu."

And so I began my new life as Betty-Fatu.

Chapter Eleven

*H*OLDING ON TO MY HAND, AAKIF WALKED UP THE
beach toward the forest. "Come. I'll take you to my village."

We left the beach and traveled through the woods. The giant oaks with their hanging moss were just as shadowy and other-worldly as I'd feared, although being with Aakif made me less afraid. He knew every twist and turn of it.

In about fifteen minutes, we came to a clearing in the oaks. Twenty small, unpainted, wooden cabins stood side by side in a straight row. They were neat but simple. Their only adornment was a bright blue outline painted around the windows and doors of each cabin.

Aakif noticed me looking at the adornment. "Ever hear of indigo?" he asked.

I had learned of it in my history lessons. "It's a dye from a plant, isn't it?"

"Besides rice, we also grow and harvest the plant it comes from, indigofera. We make it into a blue dye. The bosses don't mind if we scrape the bottom of the barrels for our own use as long as we don't take too much."

"It's very pretty," I commented.

"The purpose is not for beauty," Aakif said. "It is to keep off the juju."

"Evil spirits?" I guessed.

"Yes, witchcraft. It is everywhere. We guard against it always." He tapped the blue bead he wore around his neck. "This also keeps off the juju."

Not knowing what to say about such a superstition, I changed the subject. "Which of these cabins is yours?"

"That one," Aakif said, pointing down the line. "When I came here, I thought I would have no family, but as fortune had it, I discovered a cousin of my mother's was already here — enslaved many years ago. She is much respected as a conjuror among the bin yahs. Her name is Mother Kadiatu, but everyone calls her Aunty Honey because she keeps bees."

"Will I meet her?"

"You will. Soon. You will love her and especially her cooking. She makes the best gumbo on the island."

We walked along the cabins and I noticed that there was no one around. "Where is everyone?" I asked.

"Working," Aakif told me. "The last of the harvest is still coming in. The women are already beating the first of it that came. When the slavers are here, everyone works hard, hard. But when they leave, we let the old people and the children stay home to work at easier tasks."

"Why aren't you working?" I asked.

Aakif grinned mischievously. "When I told the other foremen that I thought I saw a forest spirit on the beach, they let me go. Now I must let Aunty Honey know that I have returned and no harm has come upon me."

"Aunty Honey is home now?"

"Yes, she is old, old, old. No one knows exactly how many years. Even Aunty Honey is not quite sure, I think."

"You said Aunty Honey is a conjuror. I've never heard that word."

Aakif stared at me with a puzzled expression. "Never heard of a conjuror?" he questioned incredulously.

"No," I replied, shaking my head.

"Aunty Honey knows how to use plants — leaves and roots — to keep off the gafa."

"Gafa?"

"The evil spirits. If someone has put the hudu on you — you know, a spell, a curse — Aunty Honey knows how to get it off. If a njoso enters you, Aunty Honey can drive it out with her medicines."

At once, I pictured Bronwyn with her herbal medicines.

"Does anyone accuse her of being a witch?" I asked.

"A witch?! Aunty Honey?! No! No!" Aakif explained, waving his hands as if to shoo the question off. "There is witchcraft on this island, but not Aunty Honey."

"Do you know who the witches are?"

"No, they keep themselves secret," Aakif replied seriously. "Sometimes you can see them at night. They fly through the sky."

Again, I thought of Bronwyn and wondered if she was still traveling.

"You can see the witches because they leave a trail of shooting lights," Aakif went on.

"I saw a shooting star last night," I recalled.

"That was a witch that you saw," Aakif insisted.

There was no point in arguing with him. He was certain of the things he believed. And besides, who was I to say he was wrong?

81

"Magic is everywhere," Aakif went on. "Every day we see magic; we live with it. The only magic that is bad is magic intended to do harm — evil magic."

"And witches do the evil magic?" I inquired.

"Yes."

I decided to keep my desire to study witchcraft a secret. It would not do me any good to have these people think I was a witch, but I wondered if I could learn anything from Aunty Honey's conjuring.

Aakif stopped in front of the last cabin on the row. When I followed him to the other side, I realized we had been walking behind the cabins. The fronts of the cabins faced a sort of village square bordered by more slave cabins on the other side.

Clustered together under a spreading oak, four white-haired men wove more of the sweet grass baskets Aakif had given me. A little way off, two elderly men sat on a simply made bench carving blocks of wood — one shaped a wooden bowl, the other whittled a wooden chain. In the center of the green, about fifteen adorable children, aged from three to ten, ran around, laughing. They seemed to be playing a game of tag. Five grandmotherly women appeared to be patching garments with needle and thread while they watched over babies who either crawled or slept on blankets near them.

"It is like a different world here when the bosses are gone,"

Aakif commented. "We are thankful for this heavy, heavy heat that drives them off for a time."

A mosquito stung my shoulder and I slapped at it, leaving a splotch of blood where it had gotten me. Now that I no longer had the cooling ocean breeze and the protection of the shady oaks, I realized how truly scorching it was.

Staggering slightly, I clutched Aakif's shoulder to keep from falling. Aakif steadied me. "Ah, Betty-Fatu, I see for certain that you are no forest spirit. You are a white and cannot stand the heat. Aunty Honey will feed you and cool you down."

With my arm draped across his shoulder for support, Aakif led me toward his cabin. As we neared, I became aware of a continuous hum and looked toward the sound. Over to the side of the last cabin where Aakif lived with Aunty Honey were six sweet grass baskets, only they were large and cone-shaped. They sat upside down on small wooden tables. There was a small hole in each one; occasionally a bee would fly in or out. "Those are Aunty Honey's bee skeps," Aakif explained as he eased me toward the steps to his cabin. "There's a real beehive in each one. Aunty Honey believes honey will cure almost anything that ails a person."

The moment I turned my attention away from the bee skeps and back to the cabin, I was faced with a person I assumed was Aunty Honey herself.

Though very short in stature, she was also wide, especially at the hips. Her plain blue skirt appeared scrubbed yet stained and it had been mended in various places. She wore a shirt with wide black stripes, and wisps of cottony white hair peeked from the black head wrap she wore. Her skin was as black as Aakif's, and her small onyx eyes gleamed angrily at me.

Feet planted on the top step, and with her hands on her hips, Aunty Honey barked furiously at Aakif in a language I assumed was Gullah, but which I couldn't begin to make sense of.

Aunty Honey turned her piercing stare back to me and the rapid-fire syllables of her unfamiliar language — words she was thinking but not voicing — flooded my mind. It was a torrent of images: a mother, a father, a husband, a girl baby born, friends, cooking, tending the baby . . . then men from a nearby tribe attacking her village. Shouting. Screams. Running, running, running through a wide savannah, howling baby clutched to her chest. A net hurtling through the air.

After that, the next images came quickly but not in the same jumbled torrent. These were horrible pictures that I didn't want to see. They rushed in just the same, and there was no way I could shut them down, even though I was trying.

Black African slaves were chained together at the ankles and wrists, packed so tightly in the lowest chambers of a ship that there was hardly enough air for them all. Aunty Honey lay shackled to another slave. The sound of wailing and anguished cries filled the space.

I saw a white man pulling at the baby girl Aunty Honey clutched. Aunty Honey screamed for her child and was hit with a metal bar from behind. I saw her crumple onto a dock where other Africans were being sold.

My mind filled with the image of Aunty Honey grinding her back molars as she was whipped by a white slaver, searing agony shooting through her. Men were nearby, laughing.

I saw things I don't ever want to see again or remember even now.

Tears flowed from me — gently at first, then harder and harder still. Rolling despair washed over me and I fell to my knees, my hands over my face, weeping from the depths of my being. Was this Aunty Honey's deep sadness or my own? I couldn't tell.

Another, different, but still overpowering emotion swept through me. Ferocious, red rage. Aunty Honey herself entered my mind, younger and stronger than she actually appeared. She glowered at me with pure hatred.

Never had this kind of malice been directed at me. It was terrifying. In my mind, I saw her grab my throat and squeeze. Each time I tried to push her off, she'd tighten her grip.

"Gafa!" Aunty Honey shrieked at me.

She tossed a white powder into my face.

The powder burned my eyes.

"Gafa! Gafa!"

From somewhere very far off, Aakif shouted urgently at Aunty Honey, speaking in the Gullah language. It was the last thing I heard before my eyes rolled up in their sockets and my knees buckled out from under me.

Chapter Twelve

WHEN MY EYES OPENED, I WAS STARING UP AT THE LEAVES of an oak. Aakif was beside me and, as I struggled up to lean on my elbows, he offered me a kind of yellow cake.

"Corn bread with honey," he explained. "Here, take it."

It was warm and wildly delicious. Aakif then handed me a carved cup filled with cool water. "She says you're a witch," he stated calmly. "She won't let you into the cabin."

I coughed up the water I had just sipped. "Why does she think I'm a witch?" I asked. Had she seen into my deepest secret, my desire to know what witches knew? Did she know about my grandmother and great-grandmother?

"Aunty Honey told me that you went into her mind and witnessed her most hidden memories. To protect her thoughts, she had to enter your mind and put a stop to it."

It was true!

"I think she was trying to kill me," I said, remembering the old woman's ferocious violence.

"No. If Aunty Honey wanted you dead, you would be dead."

We sat there for several minutes without speaking.

"Do *you* think I am a witch?" I finally asked.

It was a relief to see a smile spread across his handsome face. "Would I give you my corn bread if I did? No. I don't think there is any bad in you — but there is power, the same power as in Aunty Honey."

"How do you know that?"

Aakif shrugged. "I can feel it. Sometimes I just know things. I have . . . I don't know . . . I think the word for it is *instinct*. I have an instinct for people and what they are like. But Aunty Honey does not guess, she knows. She has great power but also knowledge. She has studied the roots and flowers, even minerals and animals."

"Where does she get her supplies?" I asked.

"Some are brought in from Africa, often already ground. Like a blowfish for instance. Did you know that the venom from a blowfish can make a person appear dead, even though that person is really still alive?"

A shiver of fear ran through me. "How awful! Has Aunty Honey ever poisoned anyone?" I asked, fearful of the answer but needing to know. If so, I would have to be careful of everything Aakif offered me to eat.

Aakif sighed and contemplated the question for a moment. "Aunty Honey boasts of poisoning many folk. All her victims had bad juju, she claims, and deserved to die."

"She thinks *I* have bad juju," I reminded Aakif.

"I know. I did not expect that when I brought you to her."

"What should I do?"

"Be careful of her," he advised. "I will speak with her on your behalf."

Leaning forward, I felt strong enough to get to my feet. "I think I should go back to the beach," I decided. "It's probably best if I stay out of Aunty Honey's way." I really didn't need her turning the whole village against me.

"Maybe so," Aakif agreed, no doubt with the same idea in mind. He went back to his cabin and quickly returned with a cloth bag. "Supplies," he explained. Swatting another mosquito, I let him lead me back the way we'd come. "Do you want to stay on the beach or in the forest?" he asked.

"The beach," I answered without thinking about it much. I simply liked the beach better. "It's cooler and has fewer mosquitoes," I added.

"The smoke from your fire will help keep them off," Aakif said. "I've brought you more coal."

Once more, we walked through the shadowy forest. I told him how I'd thought I'd seen an angel the other day, but it was a heron.

"Ah, I know of these angel spirits," Aakif said. "How do you know them?"

"From the Bible. My father would read it to us every night."

"Sometimes here on the plantation, white men in black robes come to read it to us. Mostly they read stories about Jesus. I like those stories. But I first heard of angels from the Muslims back in Sierra Leone. I met them while working for the palm oil company. Their stories are very much like the Bible stories, and they too have angels."

"I've never met a Muslim, but I've read of them. I didn't know they also have angels in their religion. It just shows you people are more alike than they realize."

"Maybe." Aakif sounded skeptical. "It's not easy to find anything in common with the plantation owner or his family or his foremen."

"What about me?" I asked quietly.

Aakif gazed into my eyes. "You're different from them."

It made me extremely happy to hear those words. "I hope so. I want to be," I said. "Tell me how I'm different."

Aakif smiled softly as he brushed some hair from my eyes. "You are njoso, Betty-Fatu, but you are not a spirit from the forest. You are an ocean sprite."

The first thing Aakif and I did when we reached the remnants of my old fire was to build a new one. After that, we set up a tent, made from a quilt that looked like it was woven but was really strips of fabric sewn together.

After that was done, we walked the shore, talking for close to an hour. His dream was to buy his freedom. The plantation owners paid their foremen a small wage. "And during the off-season sometimes I can fish and row over to the mainland after dark to sell my catch. I know a man there who takes it from me and pays right at the dock. I can be back before anyone knows I'm gone."

"Do you think you can ever earn enough?"

"Men have done it on this plantation before," Aakif replied, his voice filled with determination. "And if others have, I can."

"You'll do it," I said, feeling sure he would.

"What about you? What do you want?" he asked.

"Right now I just want to find a way home."

"When the masters return in two months, we'll make sure they help you."

Could I last two months? It seemed like such a long time to live out here on the beach by myself. But at least I had Aakif to help me.

"After you go home, I suppose you want to marry a rich man and have babies," Aakif assumed.

"No," I confessed, "that's not what I want at all. I want the independence to live as I like, to be a free woman."

This made Aakif smile. "So we have the same dream, then."

"In some ways," I agreed, returning his smile.

Returning to my beach campsite, we stoked the fire and heated Aunty Honey's famous gumbo. Then Aakif handed me a glass bead strung on a reed, like the one he wore. "To keep off the bad juju," he said.

I turned the bead over in my hand. It was a deep blue. The glass was full of air bubbles and was a little uneven, so it was obviously handblown, possibly very old. "Will I need this to protect myself from Aunty Honey?" I asked.

"I don't think so," Aakif answered, though he sounded uncertain. "She is not a bad woman, only a powerful one."

Aakif tied the beaded reed around my neck. "A girl who floated to safety across the wide ocean in a barrel most likely doesn't need a bead to help her. But just the same, I want you to have it."

After our supper, we sat by the fire, watching the waves. Aakif took hold of my hand, which thrilled me at first, but soon came to feel very natural.

"Would you like to hear a song I know?" I asked him. "I sang it while I was floating in my barrel."

"Absolutely, yes! Sing it for me."

Fighting a moment of self-consciousness, I leaned back on my arms and sang out: *"The water is wide, I can-not cross o'er. And neither have I the wings to fly . . ."*

When I was done, I asked him, "Did you like it?"

He was looking at me deeply. "Very much. If you were with me, I would never let you sink."

In my mind, I heard the end of his sentence, which he was thinking to himself. *Never ever let you sink, beautiful sea sprite. I will always take care of you.*

Squeezing his hand, I rested my head on his strong arm for just a moment before straightening again.

With a reluctant sigh, Aakif released my hand and rose to his feet. "I have to be back at the rice fields before dawn tomorrow, so I should go to sleep."

"Stay a little longer," I implored.

He sat back down beside me. "Get into the tent and sleep," he said. "I will stay here until you are safely dreaming."

I crawled into the tent with my head at the front opening. He sat cross-legged in front of me.

"I will be back as soon as I can tomorrow," he promised. "There's some bread for you still in the basket for your breakfast, and fresh water."

"Now you sing me a song," I requested.

"All right," he agreed. "Here's one from the sea islands, right here." With a deep breath, he began to sing a song in a low, plaintive voice. It was a slow, soothing song:

> *Steal away*
> *Steal away*
> *Steal away*
> *Steal away*
> *We're going home to Africa*
> *Steal away*
> *Steal away*
> *We ain't got long for stayin'. . . .*

Dropping my head, I let sleep start to carry me. *"We ain't got long for stayin',"* sung in his strong sweet voice, was still playing in my ear as I went under.

During the night, I awoke bathed in my own steaming sweat. A terrible pain crossed my head. Hot saliva rose in my mouth before my stomach lurched. Pulling myself out the front of the tent just in time, I vomited in wrenching spasms.

Aunty Honey *had* poisoned me, after all. I was sure of it.

I tossed sand over my vomit and groped in the sweet grass basket for the water Aakif had left me. But before I could even lift it to my mouth, my stomach heaved again and once more I was spilling my guts onto the sand.

Chapter Thirteen

S OMEONE'S HAND WAS ON MY FOREHEAD. "HER FEVER IS still burning." Had I heard it in my head or in my ears? I wasn't sure. Though I was half awake with my eyes still shut, I could tell it was Aakif.

"Mus tek cyear a de root fa heal de tree."

That was unmistakably Aunty Honey.

I'd been about to open my eyes, but I caught myself in time and instead kept them shut. Aunty Honey's voice had been in my ear and very close.

A tough, gnarled hand tapped my cheek, lightly at first and then a sharp slap. It was so hard that my eyes opened. Aunty Honey grinned coldly, satisfied that she'd proven I was faking.

I was inside a one-room cabin, lying on a low, wooden platform, wrapped in a blanket. Another sleeping platform lay sideways against the wall, blankets neatly folded beside it. One narrow window let a patch of sun shine into the otherwise shadowy room.

The cabin was nearly empty, except for a wide stone stove and a wooden table with a bench. Beside the stove there was one long shelf laden with cookware and dishes. There were also a number of glass jars filled with powders and dried herbs.

I realized a cool cloth had been laid across my forehead and I lifted it off. Aakif was instantly sitting at my side, offering me water. "Drink this," he instructed gently, holding the cup to my lips.

The water was sweet and I pulled back a bit, surprised.

"Honey water," Aakif explained, "from Aunty Honey's bees. It will make you strong again."

Aunty Honey stood by the bed, her expression stern and unyielding, her black, beady eyes cold, but she nodded when Aakif said the honey would strengthen me.

"What did she say about a tree?" I asked softly.

"It's a Gullah saying: You have to cure the root to heal the tree." After I'd sipped some more, Aakif took the cup away. "You have the —"

"— yellow fever," I croaked.

"That's right! I found you on the beach yesterday morning. You had passed out and I couldn't wake you."

"Yesterday?"

"Yes, I carried you here and convinced Aunty Honey to take you in. I told her you have a good heart and mean no harm to anyone."

Aunty Honey's eyes bore into me, and I didn't have the impression that she felt any kindlier to me now than she had before. Yet, looking down at myself, I saw that my dirty, ripped nightgown had been changed to a simple and rough but immaculately clean nightshirt of unbleached cotton. My hair still smelled of the ocean, but at least it had been bundled to the top of my head.

"Thank you," I said, turning to Aunty Honey. When I got no response, I turned to Aakif for help. "Would you tell her I said —"

"She knows what you said. She can speak English but she won't."

"Who could blame her?" I murmured, remembering all I'd seen in Aunty Honey's mind.

Aunty Honey's eyes might have darted in my direction for a flicker, but I couldn't be sure. I was suddenly very weak again.

Aunty Honey gestured toward the stove. "Fufu," she said to Aakif.

Aakif retrieved a bowl. "See if you can keep this down," he said, lifting a spoon of fufu to me.

It looked delicious but tasted awful. Aakif smiled when he saw my face crinkle with revulsion. "I know! I know!" He chuckled. "It's really good until Aunty puts her powders in there. I think she uses willow bark for pain relief and a plant called feverfew especially for the aching head. Ginger root helps with the rocking stomach."

"No poison?" I whispered.

"No poison," Aakif confirmed with a smile. "I watched her make it."

My attempt to smile back at him failed. I was simply too weak. Aakif was able to feed me half the bowl of fufu before I held my hand up to stop him.

"That's enough," he agreed. "We don't want you to start again."

"Start?"

"You had the black vomit." He tapped his stomach. "The blood from inside."

"My insides are bleeding?" I asked, alarmed.

"Do not worry. Aunty Honey will make you better." Aakif got up. "I have to get back to the field now. You rest."

Panic swept through me. He was leaving me alone with Aunty Honey! I gazed at him imploringly.

Aakif sighed, and his expression told me he would have stayed if he could have, but it was impossible. Turning, he spoke to Aunty Honey in Gullah. I didn't have to understand the language to know that he was politely asking her to treat me well.

In reply, Aunty Honey upbraided Aakif, shooing him toward the door as she scolded.

"She will take good care of you," Aakif told me, speaking over his shoulder as he went out.

When he was gone, Aunty Honey stayed by the door, her face immobile, staring at me.

Longing only to sleep, I couldn't relax with the old woman's eyes fixed on me. I didn't want her back in my head, wandering through my dreams as I slept, nor did I wish to enter her mind, not ever again. The need to sleep threatened to become overpowering, though. I had to fight it if I was going to shut Aunty Honey out.

Aunty Honey was still focused on me. Her eyes burned with a frightening intensity. There was a pressure forming in my head, and somehow I knew she was trying to get in. I had to block her somehow, so I filled my head with the song Aakif had sung to me:

Steal away
Steal away

Steal away
Steal away
We're going home to Africa
Steal away
Steal away
We ain't got long for stayin'.

The memory of Aakif's voice filled my mind. The crashing waves of that night made a musical background. It was the last thing I'd heard before the fever set in, and it made me happy to remember it. Shutting my eyes, I stopped worrying about Aunty Honey. The repetition of the lyrics and the soothing melody lulled me.

I dreamt I was back in a boat, about to go over a fall. I screamed until a stream of energy — like a powerful wind — lifted me and swept me to a new location.

Suddenly, I was in a jungle clearing. Aunty Honey was waiting for me there, but no longer dressed in her plain clothing. The impoverished slave woman was now regal, in an orange caftan adorned with African designs and an elegant head wrap of the same material and print. Each arm was adorned with a golden snake bracelet. She sat on a high-backed chair and gestured for me to sit on a bench beside her.

"Aunty Honey —" I began, but she stopped me.

"Here you will call me Mother Kadiatu."

"Where are we?" I asked, but she acted as though I hadn't spoken. I gazed at her face; she seemed younger. I realized that she'd spoken to me in English.

"I have seen your mind while you have slept in my home," Aunty Honey said to me. "I see that I was mistaken. You are no gafa. But inside you strong magic exists, a birthright that you must learn to use wisely."

"Can you teach me, . . . Mother Kadiatu?"

"I *must* teach. Fate has brought you across the wide sea. It has swept you to my doorstep so that you can learn to be a great sorceress. These things that have happened to you are not accidents. I throw you out but you come back. I could cast you away many, many times, and still you would return — because you must. Fate has willed it to be."

"I want to learn from you, Mother Kadiatu," I said with mounting excitement.

"You will know all I know," she promised.

Chapter Fourteen

IN THE NEXT DAYS, I IMPROVED QUICKLY. "TODAY WE START,"
Aunty Honey said to me after a week's time. She stood by
the stove in her cabin and faced me. She spoke low, fast, and,
fortunately for me, in English.

She beckoned me to join her in front of a pot of boiling water.
"Put these in the water," she instructed, lifting a delicate flower
from a glass jar vase that held a bunch of them. "Use the bulb
part of the cone grass wildflower."

"What do you use it for?" I asked.

"It will calm a crazed person and help with pains from bad

juju in the belly. If a person has been cursed with ringing in the ear, it make the bell quiet."

When I tossed the last bulb in the boiling water, Aunty Honey took hold of my arm at the elbow and rested her head on my shoulder. I took this to be a gesture of affection and it startled me. In a second, though, I realized she was speaking to me in a tone so low and secretive that I could barely make out what she was saying. Inclining my head toward her, I concentrated on her every whispered word.

"If a person eats this paste in large amount, it make him crazy in the head. He will see things that are not there, people who are not there. He may even hear words that no one speaks. He keeps eating, and he sickens. Or dies." Aunty Honey gazed at me meaningfully. "In honey, it is invisible and has no taste. In porridge and gumbo also."

Ice ran through my veins. Had I even had yellow fever?

That night, I walked on the beach with Aakif. "I am no good as a driver," he lamented. "Vandi's back hurts, so I tell him to rest and I thresh his rice until he feels better. Mariama is with child, so I take the pestle and work her rice in the mortar so she can put her feet up for a while. I am exhausted."

"You're kind," I remarked, "but can't you simply let them rest without working for them? You're the foreman, after all."

He laughed darkly. "Oh, I had better not do that. The bosses expect the work to be done while they are gone. They get very angry and punish us in terrible ways if it is not. It would be on my head if we were disciplined for a bad rice yield. I could not live with what I had done." Aakif took hold of my hand. "How was your day with Aunty Honey?"

"Busy," I replied. I told him how much she had taught me about several roots and some herbs. Then I told him about the cone grass. "Do you think it was in the gumbo?"

"No! Impossible! I ate the gumbo with you."

"That's true, you did."

"You don't think that I would —"

"No!" I cried, clasping his arm. "Of course not!"

Aakif threw his arms around me. "I would never hurt you, Betty-Fatu! Never ever. You must believe that!"

"I do! I know you wouldn't." Then I surprised even myself . . . and kissed Aakif.

He kissed me back.

We both pulled away.

And then we melted together and kissed again, this time more slowly.

In the next month, I learned more and more every day from Aunty Honey — or Mother Kadiatu, as I'd grown fond of calling her — during our private lessons. The people in the slave village were cordial to me because I came under the protection of Aakif and Aunty Honey, who were both highly regarded.

Day by day, a little more at a time, I became a part of the village community. I went with Aunty Honey as her assistant when she was called to the home of a sick or injured person. I got to know the people very well in that way.

In the evenings I attended the public singing at the center of the village, where a song leader would call out a verse of a song and the rest of the group would respond with an answering verse. I was welcomed at the fish fries that featured all the abundance of the island, cooked on an open fire, and shared by all.

Aakif and I continued our evening walks on the beach. With him, it was often the same story. He had taken the extra job of a man or woman who was unable to work. His compassionate kindness amazed me continuously.

For my part, I always had something new and exciting to report. Aunty Honey worked me hard but that was all right. I was learning, so I was happy.

"Soon you will leave me," Aakif predicted unhappily when I had finished reporting of my day with Aunty Honey.

"I won't leave!" I swore. "Do you want me to go?"

"Of course I do not!" Aakif took my hand. "It is the last thing that I want. But let me tell you a real thing, Betty-Fatu. It is the season for the white bosses to return. The happy time will be over. It will hardly seem to be the same place. You will no longer like to be here. Besides, they will see you and take you away no matter what."

I clutched Aakif's arm, pulling close to him. "No, they can't take me." The idea of leaving him filled me with panic. We had grown so close. I loved him with all my heart. I couldn't picture my life without having him to talk to every evening.

"Don't you want to see your family once more?" Aakif asked. "You must miss them."

"I do, very much, but I don't even know if I have a family any —" I couldn't continue the sentence or bear to even think it. Father and Kate had to be alive!

Just then, I heard the sound of pounding hoofbeats on the beach and turned toward it. Three men on horseback were approaching us at great speed — three white men.

Confused and panicked, I looked to Aakif.

"Don't move," he told me in a voice filled with tension.

We stood where we were as the men slowed alongside us. The lead man was tall and strongly built. He pulled a club from his saddle. "John!" he bellowed at Aakif. "What are you doing down on the beach with this —" he looked me over with distaste "— this white girl?"

"She washed ashore after a shipwreck and we have been caring for her, Mr. Parris, sir," Aakif answered evenly.

"Is that so?" Mr. Parris sneered. "And what is it that made you believe you could be going on romantic walks with this pretty little white girl?"

As he spoke, he dropped from his saddle and, with his club flailing, attacked Aakif.

"Stop that!" I screamed, flying at Parris. He pushed me back so hard that I dropped to the sand. I was scrambling to get up when each of the other men grabbed one of my arms.

Writhing violently, I squirmed to free myself from their iron grips, but with no success.

In front of me, Parris continued whaling on Aakif, who raised his arms to defend himself from the blows but could not escape the much larger man. Desperate to help him, I sank my teeth into the hand of the man grasping my right arm.

Swearing at the top of his voice, he released me, but I was still held by the man on my left. In the next second, the man I'd bitten slapped me so hard across the face that I flew from the other man's grasp.

The last thing I recall is my feet lifting from the ground and my body being hurled across the sand.

I awoke in a bed under a pink satin cover that matched the ruffled pink canopy overhead. It was a world of pink —

walls, rug, furniture, curtains. I could only open my left eye. When I gingerly touched the right side of my face, I cried out in pain.

"Stop complaining and be thankful you're alive, young lady." The woman speaking walked into view. She was in her thirties, with blond hair swept up into ringlet curls at the top of her head.

Coming close, she inspected me, then took a hand mirror from the night table and held it so I could see my own badly bruised face. "I don't know why they had to be quite so rough with you," she allowed. "But I daresay it was for your own good. You can't be cavorting on the beach with the slaves." She paused and, shutting her eyes, emphasized her point with a violent shiver of horror. "Where *can* you be from that you don't know *that?*"

"Am I a prisoner?" I asked, ignoring her question as I sat up.

She tittered with laughter. "Heavens, no! I am Mrs. Abigail Parris and you are my guest. Now that I hear you speak, I can perceive that you are from England."

"What happened to my friend, Aakif?"

The woman stared at me blankly.

"You call him John," I prodded.

"I don't really know the slaves," Mrs. Parris answered.

My body ached as I threw off the covers and swung my feet to the carpeted floor. I was still dressed in the cotton patchwork skirt and striped shirt I'd been wearing, though I could see that a ruffled nightgown had been laid out for me across a pink chaise longue.

"Where are you going? I can show you to the ladies' bathroom," the woman offered.

"I need to leave to see how my friend is."

"You're heading to the slave quarters?!" she cried in horror.

"That's where I've been living for the last month."

"Well, there will be no more of that!" Mrs. Parris stated firmly, heading toward the door. "You will stay right here until we figure out what to do with you. Don't worry. You will never step foot in those dreadful slave quarters again."

"You don't understand! I want to go back."

"You can't mean that, I'm sure," Mrs. Parris insisted. "You've been through a terrible time. Your mind isn't as it should be."

I lunged for the door, but she spun around to the hall outside and, in a second, pulled it shut. With a click, I heard it lock. Yanking at the knob did no good, so I ran to the window. Pushing aside the curtains, I could see right away that I was in the main plantation house. From where I stood, the slave cabins were barely visible through the oaks.

The brutal Mr. Parris, who had attacked Aakif, strode up the front steps. How I hated him! A large whip was coiled in his hand.

Had he used that on Aakif?

I had to find him. Flying to the bedroom door, I pulled at the crystal knob. "Let me out of here! You can't keep me locked in! Let me out!"

But no one replied.

Chapter Fifteen

FOR THE NEXT TWO DAYS, THE PARRIS FAMILY KEPT ME locked in the room, though they fed me well and attended to my injuries. They even claimed to have released from their employ the man who had hit me.

But I detested them. For the life of me, I couldn't get the image of Mr. Parris beating Aakif from my mind, nor could I abide Mrs. Parris's sugarcoated smugness.

Every time either of them entered the room, I made such a fuss that their tone with me soon became sharp and impatient — at times even threatening. They agreed to free me if

I would promise not to steal away to the slave cabins. But I couldn't promise that when my only wish on earth was to see Aakif once more. They wouldn't tell me anything of his condition. Whether I was awake or asleep, I was frantic with the fear that they had killed him.

On the third day, they roused me to tell me that Reverend Samuel Parris, a Puritan minister in Salem Village in the Massachusetts Bay Colony, and a cousin to Mr. Parris, had agreed to take me in. "He and his wife have three children and the additional care of his orphaned niece. They have need of a servant," Mrs. Parris informed me.

"A servant?" I questioned. "I am not a servant and I don't want to be one."

"Is that so? And how do you intend to pay for your meals and board?" Mrs. Parris asked coldly. "How is it that you plan to live in this world?"

The treasured image that I had in my head — the idea of working as a psychic and living independently — suddenly seemed ridiculous. Who would hire me for such work?

Without Aakif and Aunty Honey, I was alone in the world. The Parrises would never let me go back to the slave quarters, nor did they intend to extend to me the same loving care I had once known.

"Could I be a servant here?" I asked. That way at least I could find my way to Aakif.

"Ha!" Mrs. Parris barked with derision. "I should say not. We don't need a white servant here. We have all the house slaves and field slaves we require."

That very afternoon, the Parrises had two slaves row the three of us to the Charleston Harbor. There was no question of me saying good-bye to Aakif or Aunty Honey. I could not even ask.

I knew the slaves in the boat slightly from being in the village — Salifu and Bala were their names — and tried to make contact, but neither of them would risk meeting my glance. When that failed, I cast my eyes down and focused on trying to read their minds. Their thoughts were expressed in Gullah, but I was able to hear. They both pitied me but felt it was better that I was "with my own kind."

Concentrating, I tried to reach them with my own thoughts. *Aakif. What has happened to him?*

It was no use. Though I was able to hear them, they could not perceive my anxious, unspoken question.

Charleston Harbor was a busy commercial port, and our small craft was rocked in the wake of so many large ships. When Bala finally tied up the boat, getting onto the dock was not easy. Mr. Parris assisted his wife but left me to fend for myself. Salifu got on deck and extended me a helping hand. "Good-bye, Betty-Fatu," he said in English.

"Is Aakif alive?" I whispered.

"Alive, yes," he answered quietly.

"How is he?"

"Not good. Very bad." As he spoke, he took something from inside the bib front of his faded overalls and rapidly passed it to me. I dropped it into the quilted cloth bag Mrs. Parris had given me to take a few items. The quick glance I gave it told me immediately that I was holding a jar of Aunty Honey's own honey.

"Thank her," I said softly to Salifu just as Mr. Parris coughed irritably for me to join him and his wife, who had already headed up the dock.

They escorted me to a ship named the *Loyal Servant*. As we approached it, memories of the *Golden Explorer* going down brought a flutter of panic, but I was able to fight it.

"Your fare is paid and off you go," Mr. Parris said as he directed me up the gangplank. "Heed my cousin well. He is a pious man and will not take kindly to being disobeyed."

I pray he's not a slave driver like you, I thought bitterly as I walked away from them.

The salt air stung my bruises as I found myself once again on the deck of a many-sailed ship.

As I stood wondering how to get off the ship, I absently watched the people boarding. There were all sorts of types and classes of people.

For the first time, I saw one of the native Americans, a man with long black hair tied at the base of his neck. A young woman with him seemed to be his daughter. I was fascinated by them and tried to read into their minds, but could not decode the language that they spoke.

A priest in a black cassock with a white collar was next to walk up the gangplank. Behind him, two of the ship's crew members carried a pallet on which what appeared to be a very still body was blanketed, mummy-like, and strapped on. Two nuns walked behind the body. They kept their hands on their high wimples so they wouldn't blow away. The rosary beads at their waists also lashed back and forth in the wind as did their long dresses, one brown, the other blue.

Was the figure on the pallet dead and being brought home to bury? The idea of a dead body being on the ship gave me gooseflesh. I turned away from it.

"Last call for all passengers!" a crewman called from the top of the ship. I was on my way to Salem to be a servant, no matter if I wished to or no.

On the first day out, I was watching the white-capped ocean roll by when the nun dressed in blue approached me. She clutched a book to her side and I noticed its title was in Spanish: *El Castillo Interior*. Father had insisted that, from a young age, Kate and I study several languages, and Spanish was among them. I could translate the title: *The Interior Castle*.

The nun greeted me, her veil flapping like a sail.

"Good morning to you, Sister. My name is . . ." Here I hesitated. How did I want to introduce myself? "My name is Betty-Fatu," I continued without further hesitation. In my heart, I knew that forevermore it would always be my name.

"I am Sister Mary Carmen. Pleased to meet you," she replied, her English accented with Spanish.

"How do you like your book, Sister?" I asked.

Sister Mary Carmen's smile became radiant. "Very wonderful! It is by Saint Teresa of Avila."

"What's it about?" I asked.

"Saint Teresa was very holy, and loved God very much," Sister Mary Carmen began. "One day she had a vision from God. She saw a large crystal egg, and in it were seven mansions."

"She actually saw this?" I asked. I wondered if it might have been a dream.

Sister Mary Carmen nodded seriously. "Saint Teresa was a great mystic. She went into trances of ecstasy in which she experienced direct contact with God's love. They say she seemed to be somewhere else altogether. I often wonder if her soul traveled. Personally, I believe it must have risen out of her physical being."

Of course I thought of Bronwyn and the times I'd seen her so limp and deeply asleep as though her soul was — as she'd claimed — truly elsewhere.

"I'm sure she was," I said.

Sister Mary Carmen opened her book and perused it. "And there was something else mysterious about Saint Teresa," she said, and then hesitated, as though considering whether or not to speak the next words on the tip of her tongue.

"Tell me," I prodded.

"Sometimes she levitated," Sister Mary Carmen whispered.

I wasn't sure I'd heard her correctly. Could it be? "Do you mean she floated in air?"

Sister Mary Carmen nodded, her eyes wide with the importance of what she'd just imparted. "That's what people reported. They claimed to have seen her rise from the ground when she was in a deep trance."

My next words were so bold, I couldn't believe I was actually speaking them.

"Did anyone accuse her of being a witch?"

To my surprise and relief, Sister Mary Carmen did not seem offended by my question. "They did, in a way," she replied. "Some of her friends suggested that her visions might be coming from the Devil and not from God at all."

"Did they try to hurt her?"

"Saint Teresa did it to herself. She punished herself in various ways to drive out the Devil if he was indeed in her. She stopped only when a priest told her he was sure her visions and trances were from God. I admire her so much."

"Saint Teresa sounds like an interesting woman," I said. A person who would punish herself was a little unnerving to me, but I had to admire her dedication.

"Very interesting," Sister Mary Carmen agreed. "She was a scholarly and independent woman all the way back in the fifteen hundreds."

Sister Mary Carmen was not what I expected a nun to be like. I found her easy to talk to. "Why did you become a nun?" I asked.

Sister Mary Carmen's forehead wrinkled as she considered this question. "Since I have not yet taken my final vows, there is still time to change my mind," she said. "So I am thinking about this quite a lot. The right reason to become a nun is because your love for God is so great that you want to dedicate your life to Him. And I am not sure I have this calling."

"Then why are you doing it?"

Sister Mary Carmen came closer to me and inclined her head so she could speak confidentially. "To be a nun has its benefits. It's not quite an independent life, but as a nun, I can continue to study and I can be of service to the world. I want to learn medicine and to heal. I feel that my calling is as a healer, and as a nun I can do that. I can have a bigger life than I would otherwise have."

I clutched her arm. "I know how you feel!" I said. "It's the same reason I want to be a witch."

The nun's jaw dropped at this. "No! Not a witch! Do not say so. The Devil is a witch's master."

"I mean no harm, but I want to have the power," I explained. "I want nothing to do with any Devil."

"Then do not call yourself a witch. You know what the fate of a witch can be. You do not want that."

"Then what should I call myself?"

"I don't know," Sister Mary Carmen admitted. "But I have the power in my hands. That much I know for certain. As a girl, I dreamt I lay asleep on a beach on my back with my hands up. Lightning came from the sky and split, traveling into each of my open palms. Ever since then, I've had the power. When I lay my hands on a creature that is ill, that creature — human or animal — improves."

"Can you make them ill in the same way?" I wondered.

"I would never do that. I have never even tried."

"Have you tried to help the person on the pallet?"

"Father Bernard would never allow it. We are taking her to see some doctors associated with Harvard College. There are expert doctors and men of science at Harvard who know all about this kind of sleeping sickness. This is the first ship that would take us, so we are docking in Salem rather than in Boston Harbor."

"What's wrong with your patient?" I asked.

"It's a most unusual case. She was found floating on a ship's wreckage, unconscious and assumed dead. But she stirred, only a bit, and even now clings to life by the merest thread."

Every nerve in my body suddenly buzzed with excitement. "Please, you must let me see her!"

Sister Mary Carmen glanced quickly around the deck. "It might be possible if we can avoid Father Bernard."

"What's the patient's name?" I asked, hungry to know.

"We have no idea," Sister Mary Carmen answered. "None at all."

Chapter Sixteen

WITH A POUNDING HEART, I FOLLOWED SISTER MARY Carmen down to the lower deck where her patient lay, still on her pallet, unconscious. The older nun, Sister Costancia, sat slouched against a wall, snoring loudly.

My breath caught in my throat. "Bronwyn!" I gasped.

Sister Mary Carmen whirled toward me in shocked surprise. "You know this woman?"

Rushing to Bronwyn, I knelt at her side. There was life in her! "She has been my governess since I was born. We were lost at sea when the *Golden Explorer* sank. We have to get her above deck."

"But it's windy and cold there," Sister Mary Carmen said. "Wouldn't she be better here?"

"No! No! She is searching for herself!" Without waiting for Sister Mary Carmen, I grabbed Bronwyn under her arms and began to lift.

"No, pick up the entire pallet," Sister Mary Carmen advised. "It will be easier." Each of us took an end and lifted.

Carrying Bronwyn was alarmingly easy — she had lost a great deal of weight in the time since the wreck. "Has she been eating?"

"We get broths and other liquids into her," Sister Mary Carmen replied, "but that's all."

We bumped and banged our way out of the tiny room, fortunately not waking Sister Costancia, although she sputtered and repositioned herself several times.

"Betty-Fatu, Father Bernard will not be pleased about this," Sister Mary Carmen said as she hoisted Bronwyn and her pallet up the hatch while I pushed from below. "What will I tell him? Why are we doing this? I don't really understand."

I climbed above while Sister Mary Carmen pulled Bronwyn away to the side. As soon as I caught my breath, I explained. "Bronwyn's body has been separated from her spirit for a long time. Her spirit is searching and needs to return to her body."

With serious eyes, Sister Mary Carmen searched my face, deciding what to think of such fantastic words. "My mother claimed to travel on the astral plane," she said at last. "I never knew whether to believe her or not."

"It's real," I said. And instantly I doubted my own verification; I wasn't sure my experience was authentic, and not a dream or delirium. "I think it's real, anyway," I amended. "I hope it is."

"I hope so too," Sister Mary Carmen said.

We carried Bronwyn to a side of the ship that was relatively quiet and unvisited by crew or passengers and set her down next to a cabin wall. Although I knew I would not see it with my eyes, I gazed to the sky searching for some sign of Bronwyn's spirit presence.

Turning my sight back to Bronwyn, I was appalled at how wan and brittle she appeared. Her closed eyes were sunken; her skin had a translucence that gave the impression that one was seeing the skeleton below. It terrified me to see my earthy, vibrant governess looking so fragile and gray.

"I'll be right back," I said as I ran for my bag, which I'd stashed beside some barrels. I returned instantly and dug out my jar of honey. Sister Mary Carmen cast a quizzical glance my way.

I dashed a finger of honey into my mouth and offered the jar to Sister Mary Carmen, who did the same. The honey's sweet goodness suffused me and I was sure Bronwyn would benefit from it. "How should I feed this to her?" I asked.

Pulling a clean white handkerchief from her sleeve, Sister

Mary Carmen swiped it through the honey and then put it to Bronwyn's lips.

"What is the meaning of this?" Father Bernard towered above us, his cassock tossed behind him by the wind.

Sister Mary Carmen inclined her head respectfully toward him. "Please forgive us, Father, but this is Betty-Fatu, and our patient is her governess."

The balding priest assessed me with his piercing eyes. "What sort of name is Betty-Fatu?" he inquired of me.

"In England, my name was Elsabeth James," I replied, getting to my feet. "Betty-Fatu is a nickname bestowed on me by a loving friend."

Father Bernard nodded, his expression still stern, and inquired why we had moved the patient.

"I thought the fresh air might do her good," Sister Mary Carmen fibbed on my behalf.

"See that she's never alone," the priest commanded before he left us.

Sister Mary Carmen breathed out a gust of relief. "That went better than I would have expected."

Whenever the weather was fair, Sister Mary Carmen and I carried Bronwyn's senseless body out on deck, bundled in blankets for warmth. Her limp form worried me tremendously.

Only the honey we fed her seemed to rouse any color to her cheeks.

Sitting on the deck by Bronwyn's pallet, I spoke to her in a low, confiding voice, hoping to reach something inside that might prevent her from slipping away altogether. I also wanted to occupy my mind so I wouldn't long for Aakif, whom I missed so deeply, and Kate and Father, lest I be filled with an inconsolable sadness.

Sometimes I would try to use my power of mind reading to search into Bronwyn's inner thoughts. All that came to me was a whooshing sound, like wind, and a thumping like distant thunder. Was all that remained of Bronwyn breath and heartbeat? It seemed so.

One morning, as I was keeping my vigil, Sister Mary Carmen came to sit beside me as she usually did, but this morning she was especially animated.

"I have been thinking," she told me. "If we sang very loudly, would it help attract Bronwyn's attention? Might it guide her to her body?"

"It sounds possible," I said.

"Is there a song she would recognize as coming from you?"

For a moment I looked blankly at my friend, not sure what to answer. But then I tossed my head back, singing "The Water Is Wide" at full volume into the wind.

My voice croaked and tears welled as I sang the verse, *"Build me a boat that can carry two, and both shall row, my true love and I."* It made me long for Aakif. Where was he now? Was he all right?

As I repeated the song again and again, striving to sing above the wind, my voice picked up strength. I scanned the sky as I sang, searching for any sign of Bronwyn. Could I really sing her down out of whatever astral plane she was now on?

By sunset that night, I had sung the song without stop until my throat was a rasp. Sister Mary Carmen brought me a bowl of chicken broth from the ship's galley and insisted I eat. As I devoured the golden soup, she took up the song, taking it an octave higher in a voice of pure crystalline beauty.

Finishing the soup, I set the bowl aside and sat mesmerized by the loveliness of Sister Mary Carmen's voice. The daylong vigil of song had left me weary, and I laid my head on Bronwyn's bony shoulder and drifted into sleep.

When I woke, I saw that it was fully night. Sister Mary Carmen's otherworldly singing still filled the air.

Something in the sky caught my attention. A shooting star arced, sparking through the blackness. And then another and another. My father would have called it a meteor shower.

Instantly, I was on my feet, clutching Sister Mary Carmen's wrist and pointing to the lights. "It's her! She's found us! Sing louder!"

Together we raised our voices to top volume, straining to sing even louder. The shooting stars shot through the sky ever lower and larger to our sight.

"Put your hands on her," I urged Sister Mary Carmen.

Still singing, Sister Mary Carmen knelt beside Bronwyn, one hand on the top of Bronwyn's hair, the other on her bony chest.

The lights in the sky blinked out.

Turning, I was in time to see Bronwyn's eyes open. I knelt at her side. "Bronwyn, you're back," I sobbed. "You're back."

"Do I know you?" Bronwyn whispered, her voice low and hoarse.

"It's me, Elsabeth!"

Bronwyn sat up and her eyes shone with a ferocity I had never witnessed before — not from her, nor from any other living creature. The blue of her eyes appeared to spin, rotating ever faster.

I froze, mesmerized by the sight, unsure if what I was seeing was real.

What remained after the spinning ceased was a void, as though there were no eyeballs in her sockets at all. Her eyes were completely black.

Jerking back in terror, I looked to Sister Mary Carmen, but she was paralyzed with fear, mouth agape.

"Bronwyn, what's wrong?" I shouted.

Pivoting toward me, Bronwyn opened her mouth as though to scream, but no sound emerged from her mouth.

Alarmed, I looked once more to Sister Mary Carmen and saw that she was clutching her ears, cringing in horrible pain.

In the next second, I heard it too. Screaming filled my head as though a thousand voices howled in unbearable pain while another thousand moaned in despair. The sound became so shrill the vibration caused my bones to quake.

Bronwyn rolled from the mat and in an instant was standing.

Father Bernard turned the corner and witnessed Sister Mary Carmen and me writhing in pain. His eyes darted to Bronwyn and he tensed.

He spoke urgently to Sister Mary Carmen and me, but the sound in my head was so great I couldn't hear his words.

Father Bernard grabbed my arm and that of Sister Mary Carmen, yanking us away from Bronwyn before hurling us even farther down the deck. The screaming dimmed enough for me to hear his words. "Get away from her. Stay away!"

Bronwyn glowered at the priest, her eyes radiating fiery pin-pricks at the center of their blackness.

Father Bernard lunged at her, grabbing her shoulders, but Bronwyn lifted him effortlessly above her head.

I was thrown across the bow of the ship as it spun counter-clockwise at an incredible speed. I hit the deck hard and then slid, banging off the sides of ropes and barrels, unable to regain my footing.

I screamed as Father Bernard hurtled over my head, his arms and legs flailing.

"Father!" Sister Mary Carmen screamed, reaching out. But she was unable to help him, since she too was sliding across the ship.

Father Bernard hit the side wall of the ship at incredible speed and was shot into the air, falling down into the black ocean below.

And then everything was suddenly quiet and still.

Bronwyn stood with her arms folded, seemingly unfazed by the ship's bizarre spin. Her eyes had returned to their blue, but there was none of Bronwyn's warmth in them.

They were the coldest eyes I had ever seen.

Chapter Seventeen

$\mathcal{A}$ MAN OVER!" THE FIRST MATE BELLOWED, RUSHING TO the side of the ship and peering over. Sister Mary Carmen and I followed him but spied no sign of Father Bernard.

The captain assigned crew members to check for structural damage to the ship and told the passengers not to worry. My eyes were riveted on Bronwyn the entire time and I was sure I saw her lips twist into the slightest smirk as the captain spoke. I had never before seen her wear such a contemptuous expression.

The father and daughter who had boarded in Charleston were also staring at Bronwyn. When Bronwyn sensed their gaze, she snapped around in their direction. The father wrapped a protective arm around his daughter's shoulder and hurried away with her.

Without a word to us, Bronwyn headed belowdecks.

As everyone slowly dispersed, Sister Mary Carmen and I stayed at the side of the ship, watching vigilantly for any sight of Father Bernard. "What have we done? What's happened?" I asked.

"Maybe the weather caused the spin," Sister Mary Carmen suggested hopefully.

"You know that's not so. You saw what happened. She is completely changed. She raised me since I was born and — you saw — she didn't even recognize me."

Sister Mary Carmen sighed in distress. "Well, she has been asleep for a very long time. It could be that her mind is not right."

"But her eyes! And what was that screaming?"

"Perhaps she has a medical condition due to her long sleep."

"And the screaming?"

Crossing herself, Sister Mary Carmen said a prayer for Father Bernard's soul as tears came to her eyes.

Putting my arms around her, I murmured my condolences. "I am going to check on Bronwyn," I said, thinking Sister Mary Carmen might want a moment alone with her grief.

As I headed belowdecks, I fought down an inexplicable sensation of growing dread. It was silly, I told myself. This was

Bronwyn, after all, dear Bronwyn who was like a mother to me. She was simply changed — as Sister Mary Carmen had suggested — by spending such a long time in an unconscious state. The separation of her body from her soul for so long a period had altered her in strange ways, perhaps, but still, she had just now awakened. By morning she might be recovered.

I found Sister Costancia once more asleep against the wall. Bronwyn lay in Sister Costancia's narrow cot with her back to me. The slow rise and fall of her back made me sure she was sleeping.

The ship rocked and I held onto the doorjamb to steady myself. Sister Costancia listed to her right and then fell out of her chair. Hurrying to help her, I recoiled in surprised horror.

Two streams of blood ran from Sister Costancia's nose. Her eyes snapped open and there was a milky glaze over them. Kneeling to feel her pulse, I quickly knew she was dead.

We docked at the Port of Salem on a gray, rainy day in mid-November. Nearly everyone on board was ill with dysentery. It had killed a number of passengers and crew members. The cause of Sister Costancia's death was never determined.

Bronwyn had stayed on her cot for the remainder of the voyage. I watched her with increasing dismay as her altered personality did not show signs of fading away. She awoke at noon each day and ate the bowl of broth I brought her without saying anything to me and then resumed her endless sleep. It was as though she was in a waking but still comatose state. All her former emotion and warmth had deserted her. In its place was an iciness that frightened and pained me to my very depths.

If not for the companionship of Sister Mary Carmen, I don't know that I could have survived the journey. I had lost everyone I loved: Father, Kate, Aakif, and now Bronwyn. My former governess was so transformed that she was as good as gone, but having the image of her there in the flesh on a daily basis made it twice as hard. Each day I awoke hoping to see her smile and hear her lilting voice, only to be met with the same stone visage and fierce eyes.

Just before we were about to disembark, Sister Mary Carmen took hold of my elbow. "I've made a decision," she said seriously. She pulled her veil off, revealing curly black hair cut to her chin. "I am not going forward with this idea of becoming a nun. My calling is not authentic, and to proceed just so I can use my healing powers is not right."

"Are you certain?" I asked her.

"Very certain. From now on don't call me Sister, only Mary Carmen."

"All right," I agreed, "if you're sure."

Mary Carmen left to gather her belongings, preparing to disembark, and I did the same. I didn't have much, so I planned to be done quickly and then go to help Bronwyn. I had no idea where she would go, since she had no money. My only idea was to ask Reverend Parris to help me in that regard. He was a man of God, after all, and hopefully charitable.

Mary Carmen returned before I'd even begun to pack, alarm written across her face. "She's gone! I've looked all over. She's disappeared."

Instantly, I bolted past her in search of Bronwyn, racing to the galley, the captain's quarters, and then above deck. The gangplank was out and so I looked down at the busy streets of Salem Town.

"There she is!" I cried to Mary Carmen, pointing at the figure of Bronwyn moving serenely through the bustling crowd below, wearing the white nightgown she'd worn through the entire voyage.

Without a second thought, I bounded down the gangplank and darted through the crowd, running to catch up with her, shouting her name.

At a corner nearly two blocks from the dock, I caught sight of her and ran as fast as I was able, maneuvering around a man pushing a wheelbarrow, a woman selling bread, and a dog. "Bronwyn, stop!" I shouted.

Bronwyn ceased her progress and turned back toward me. I slowed, panting, about three yards away from her. But then I froze altogether. The look on her face was so filled with cruelty and hatred that I was afraid to go any nearer.

We faced each other for a long minute, our eyes locked. I couldn't move.

Once more, her eyes rotated, and when they settled, they were flooded with blackness.

The screaming began in my head, the same as before.

I crashed to my knees and closed my eyes.

It was only when the noise was finally over and my head rang with pain that I opened my eyes again. Mary Carmen's face hovered above me. "What happened, Betty-Fatu?"

Pulling myself up, I rubbed my head. "She stopped me with her eyes." It was the only way I could describe it.

"What? How? That's impossible!"

Mary Carmen was right, of course. And yet it had happened. It had been so powerful, enough to drop me to the ground.

The memory of Bronwyn's face swam in front of me. In that moment I knew something so dreadful it caused cold gooseflesh to crawl up my arms.

"Mary Carmen," I said slowly. "That is not Bronwyn."

"What?" Mary Carmen gasped. "Surely it is!"

"No. It's not," I insisted. "We have called down something evil and set it loose here in Salem."

Chapter Eighteen

WHEN MARY CARMEN AND I WERE NEARLY BACK TO THE ship, we saw the captain pointing at us. Next to him was a tall man with very dark hair that fell to his shoulders. He wore a high, starched white collar above a brown cloak. His breeches were buckled at his knees and he wore brown boots, also buckled. His demeanor was stern and he scowled at Mary Carmen and me as we approached.

"You girls should not have run off like that," the captain upbraided us. "I almost had to tell Reverend Parris here that I had lost his new servant."

Reverend Parris gazed at me sourly. "So you are Elsabeth James, the shipwrecked waif they call Betty-Fatu." I detected a British accent when he spoke.

"Yes, sir, I am she, and this is my friend Mary Carmen. Are you from England, sir?"

"I was born in London. I hear from your speech that you are also from England. I am done with it now. America is the anointed nation of the future." He looked to Mary Carmen. "Where are you headed, young woman?"

"Her two traveling companions died during the crossing and she has no place to go," I jumped in.

"Yes, the captain has informed me of the ominous troubles at sea. I am especially disturbed by the event near the Isle of Devils. That name has not fallen to the Bermudas by accident. It is an area of the Americas where the Devil has made a portal for himself whereby he may more easily transport onto the earthly plane."

His words sent shivers up my spine. Was that what had happened?

"We are God-fearing people here in Salem," Reverend Parris continued. "Puritans have come to this land to create a shining city on a hill, a beacon of godliness free of the corruptions of Catholicism and the Church of England."

Mary Carmen and I exchanged a darting glance. Since Mary Carmen was Catholic and I had been raised in the Church of England, this wasn't auspicious for us.

"Charity compels me to find a living situation for you, Mary Carmen. As the ordained minister of Salem Church, I know several families who are in need of servants."

The captain offered Reverend Parris a list of passengers. "Please initial, sir, to prove you have taken custody of these young ladies."

Reverend Parris drew in a long breath as he initialed the passenger list. "The stench of evil is in the air," he remarked.

"It's the dysentery," the captain corrected. "It's a pretty horrendous journey in that regard." He turned toward Mary Carmen. "What has become of your patient?"

"She is so very improved that she walked off the ship of her own accord," Mary Carmen replied. "We were just now trying to retrieve her, but she has eluded us."

"I'll send some crewmen out to search for her and get word to Reverend Parris when we find her," the captain offered. "Has she any family here in Salem?"

"None," Mary Carmen replied.

"But by coincidence she is my governess and is like family to me," I added. "We were sailing on the *Golden Explorer* when it went down and have been separated until now."

"You were?" the captain questioned. "I heard that no passengers survived that unfortunate wreck."

Tears jumped to my eyes. "None at all?" I asked.

"That's the story they gave us."

Reverend Parris noticed my tears. "Why are you distressed?"

"My father and sister were also on the ship, and I have been hoping that they are alive," I answered.

"Hoping does not make it so," Reverend Parris said coldly. "Each man and woman's destiny is preordained by God. If a man or woman behaves in a godly manner, God will bless him or her. If he or she does not live in accordance with God's law, then God withholds His blessings."

Red temper burned in my cheeks. "I assure you, Reverend, my father and sister were the kindest, most wonderful people imaginable."

"And I assure you, Miss Betty, that —"

"Betty-Fatu," I corrected him.

He raised an eyebrow, glaring down at me with annoyance. "And what sort of name is Fatu?"

"African."

Reverend Parris's eyes went wide with disapproval. "Ah, yes, my cousin wrote me of your time spent with the Africans. We cannot hold it against you since you were stranded, but you will bear no heathen name in my household. Miss Betty you shall be. My own daughter Elizabeth is called Betty."

Reverend Parris summoned us to follow him to a wagon pulled by a chestnut horse beside the dock. Reverend Parris waved to the driver, a tall, strongly built man with jet-black hair and tan skin. "My slave John Indian will take us to the parsonage," Reverend Parris said as he headed toward the carriage.

Mary Carmen also walked toward the carriage, but I was too distracted to follow. I had spied a ship one berth over that was unloading its cargo.

Human cargo.

Ten African men and women, mostly young, descended the gangplank, hands bound in front of them and linked together by a rope. The sight of people being treated in this way was more than I could bear.

To my added dismay, I suddenly realized that some of the enslaved were familiar to me. Bala and Salifu, who had rowed me to Charleston, were barefooted and shirtless. Also there were young women I had shared meals with and sung the call and response rounds with in the evenings: Mariama, Hawa, Jilo, and Isata.

And then my heart surged in my chest with a mixture of complete joy and utter horror.

The last to emerge from the ship was Aakif!

With my mind on nothing else, I ran to the slave ship, calling his name.

Aakif looked toward my voice. Seeing me, his face broke into radiance.

My love! My friend!

"Betty-Fatu!" Aakif shouted joyfully.

"Aakif!" I cried out, waving.

Suddenly, my shoulder was wrenched back painfully. Reverend Parris's face came in close to mine. "Don't you ever humiliate me like this again," he hissed, red with fury, "or I will pitch you out onto the road and from the pulpit I will bid all God-fearing Puritans not to take you in. You can beg for your supper, but no supper will you receive."

I twisted toward Aakif but Reverend Parris's grip was unbreakable.

Aakif was being carried off in an open cart along with the other nine. His eyes were locked on me, and there was such pain in them.

With a harsh yank, Reverend Parris pulled me away, toward the waiting carriage.

Chapter Nineteen

$\mathcal{A}$T FIRST I WAS SO DOWNCAST THAT EVEN THOUGH WE traveled through the busy streets, I didn't see much of Salem Town. Mary Carmen had figured out the cause of my sorrow because I had told her of my past and how I'd come to be in Salem. She kept a consoling hand on my arm all the while.

As we went, I couldn't help but be aware that the stores and taverns of the dirt streets were becoming less densely spaced. Soon we were in farm country. It was breathtakingly beautiful land, though the buildings were plain and wooden, often unpainted, lacking any ornamentation or charm. Likewise, the people we passed were plainly dressed in brown and white. The women all wore white bonnets.

The reverend's parsonage was built of wood and sat on a low hill. It was three stories high and had a chimney at the center of the gabled roof. A large maple sat to the side, its red and orange autumn leaves almost completely stripped bare.

We were brought in and introduced to Reverend Parris's wife, Elizabeth, a stern, unsmiling woman, and their three children — Thomas, the oldest at eleven; nine-year-old Betty; and a toddler named Susannah. While Susannah played on a straight-backed, uncomfortable-looking couch, the two older children stood with their eyes cast down and their arms to their sides. Despite the presence of children, I could tell this was a household with little laughter in it.

"Hello. My name is also Betty," I introduced myself to the pretty little girl with blond ringlets.

She continued to gaze down at her plain brown boots, refusing to look at me.

"Elizabeth, I heard a most interesting thing while in town," Reverend Parris addressed his wife. "My father's former associate, the cloth merchant Antonie Van Leeuwenhoek, has come to Salem on business, and I am considering offering him my hospitality on my father's behalf."

"I know Mr. Van Leeuwenhoek!" I cried excitedly, thinking of how he might help me find my way back to England. At the least, he might have news of my father and Kate. "Could we go there?" I begged Reverend Parris. "He could possibly assist me in getting home."

Reverend Parris's expression clouded as he considered this. "You were promised to me as a servant. My cousin has traded your service in exchange for payment of a debt he owes me."

I couldn't believe it. "He had no right to give me to you."

"Of course he did. Are you not his indentured servant? I have a sugar plantation in Barbados and there it is common practice to give servants in payment of debt. My cousin knows this."

"No!" I cried. "I am no indentured servant."

Reverend Parris dismissed my worries with a wave of his hand. "Let us not trifle over this now. You and Mary Carmen here will have a means to an honorable livelihood and that is what truly matters."

"I will prepare the house for your associate's arrival," Elizabeth Parris said to her husband.

"No. Maybe not," Reverend Parris considered. "On second thought, he has become a man of science and may no longer be a man of religion. It would not do to have him in this house."

"Please let me seek him out!" I implored passionately.

He scowled at me severely. "Speak no more of it."

I was about to entreat him again when he turned away from me to speak to his wife. "I will bring Mistress Mary Carmen to meet Thomas Putnam," Reverend Parris told his wife. "He has need of a serving girl."

Mary Carmen and I flew at each other, hugging. Our lovely friendship was coming to an end — at least temporarily. I didn't know what I would do in this foreign place without her to talk to. "Be calm, young mistresses," Elizabeth Parris counseled, gently pulling us apart. "You will see each other again at market and other places."

That was a consolation; I hoped it was true. "See you soon, Betty-Fatu," Mary Carmen bid me with sadness as Reverend Parris steered her out the door. Leaning close, she whispered, "We will find a way to contact your Dutch friend. Be assured."

I nodded and was indeed assured. I'd grown to trust Mary Carmen as a true and resourceful friend. Together we would come up with some plan. Waving once more, I watched her depart with Reverend Parris.

Mrs. Parris led me into the kitchen where I met a very beautiful native Indian woman with light brown skin and thick black hair caught up in a topknot. I guessed that she might be around thirty. "This is Tituba, our house slave," Mrs. Parris said.

Tituba nodded to me with grave dignity. Her high-boned face revealed nothing of what her inner thoughts might be.

"Tituba and her husband, John Indian, originally worked as slaves on our sugar plantation in Barbados," Mrs. Parris added.

"We brought them to Salem with us when the reverend decided to move his commercial interests to Boston, and then later when we came here so he could pursue his ministerial calling."

The word *slave* hit me with all its force. How could these Puritans think of themselves as so godly, yet still keep people in slavery? The hypocrisy was more than I could stand. I was sickened by it.

Mrs. Parris conducted me up three flights of stairs to where the rooms were much smaller and the ceiling lower. The quarters were unpainted and plain. Much of the space was taken up with shelves laden with supplies — pots, dishes, and the like. "These are the servant's quarters," she announced. "We have made space for you in Althea's room."

We entered a room barely large enough for the two narrow beds and one dresser. On the right-hand bed, two young girls sat together. They had an odd deck of cards spread out on the bed.

One was a pretty girl of about ten, with dark, expressive eyes. She possessed delicate, slim bones and was dressed plainly in brown with an apron. "This is Althea Delaney," Mrs. Parris explained. "We are hosting her while her mother recovers. Her role is to be playmate to my daughter Betty."

The other girl was rather plump and about eleven, with pointy features and light brown, wavy hair. Her dress was also brown, the material finely woven. "Betty, this is my niece, Abigail."

Althea greeted me with a sunny smile that I found very endearing. Abigail also smiled, but I found her expression to be almost arrogant, with something that struck me as insincere and made me feel she was not to be trusted. I attempted to read into her mind. I heard the words, *Must not let her see the cards.*

My eyes darted to the spread-out deck on the bed. Mrs. Parris followed my glance and was immediately alarmed. She seized upon them, appalled by what she saw. "Are these . . . these . . . fortune-telling cards?" she demanded, scooping them up.

"I want to find out what my future husband will be like," Abigail spoke brashly.

"Where did you get these?" Mrs. Parris demanded.

"In the rye field."

"The rye field! Here?! At the parsonage? These cards were in our very yard?"

Abigail nodded. "I think they belong to Tituba. She has a deck like that."

Mrs. Parris took Abigail by the arm and dragged her quickly down the hall. I looked to Althea, who seemed frightened.

"I told her we should give those back to Tituba," she said.

"What will happen now?" I asked.

"Depends on if Missus tells Reverend Parris. He'll beat Tituba if he knows those devil cards were in the house. But Mrs. Parris doesn't always report every disturbance to him."

"Why do you call them devil cards?" I asked.

Althea shrugged her slim shoulders. "I don't know. That's what the Parrises think of them. I don't see any harm in it, but anything to do with magic bothers them a lot. It's against their Puritan religion."

From downstairs, I could hear the shrillness of Mrs. Parris's scolding. Though I couldn't discern her exact words, her fury was fierce.

"That's good," Althea told me, relief in her voice. "Once Mrs. Parris gets it out, she doesn't tell the reverend. When she complains to him, the punishment is much, much worse."

I couldn't help but wonder what kind of household I had fallen into.

That night I went to bed heavyhearted and exhausted from the work that the Parrises had put me to right away. After scrubbing the kitchen floor, I was assigned to clean the wooden counters in the kitchen. I fed the chickens their evening meal and then assisted Tituba in winding sheep's wool on a card. Supper was a watery stew, which I ate with Althea, Tituba, and John Indian in the kitchen. We ate in near silence, each of us tired from the day's toils.

By the time I was dismissed, all I could think about was sleeping. Sweet, young Althea Delaney slept on the bed across from me, twisting and turning in her restless slumber. I wondered if the light from the full moon pouring onto her bed was keeping her from settling down.

Despite my deep fatigue, sleep wouldn't come to me. My mind was whirling with thoughts of everything that had happened. A million questions plagued me.

How would I find Aakif again? Was he being beaten? Where was he? Was he thinking of me as I was him? I attempted to use my powers to reach his thoughts, but I couldn't connect.

And what of Bronwyn? If she had truly been possessed of a demon, where was the real Bronwyn's spirit? Was it trapped in her body as well? Was it stranded still on the astral plane?

Were Father and Kate indeed lost at sea?

How could I make my way into Boston to contact Van Leeuwenhoek? Would he even remember me? Would he be willing to help me even if I could get to him?

My small room seemed airless and too tight. Pulling on the flat, black shoes Aunty Honey had given me, I pulled my blanket around my shoulders and padded softly out of my room and down to the first floor. Finding my way through the dark but moonlit parsonage to the kitchen, I slipped quietly out the back door.

It was late November and the air was crisp with the snap of coming winter. Pulling the blanket more closely around me, I shivered in the wind as it ruffled all the bare treetops and dried grasses.

The area around the house was a rather small, cleared space with several sheds, an open-sided lean-to filled with various cooking tools and supplies, a chicken coop, and a rustic outdoor table. Several yards behind that, the edges of a grain field abutted the yard.

There was an ominous rustling, louder than even the wind. In the dark it was hard to tell, but I assumed the rustling was from the husks of withered rye, since I'd seen a lot of brown rye fields on our way in.

As I moved around toward the front of the parsonage, I stopped short and then ducked back into a shadow. Awash in moonlight, Bronwyn was standing in the road, wearing a black cape with the hood pulled up. An immense black dog was beside her, snarling and baring its terrifying fangs. Even from my distance I could hear the menacing rumble of its growl. Both Bronwyn and the dog stared fiercely at the parsonage.

Three more women, all in hooded black capes, came down the road. White hair flowed from the side of one woman's hood. The second woman seemed young, and the third was of middle age.

The three women stood in a line behind Bronwyn and the snarling hound. In unison, they raised their arms, intoning an ominous chant that I could not understand.

The ground under me vibrated and the shutters on the parsonage window clacked as they banged against the outside walls.

I knelt low, terrified that they might notice me observing their weird ritual. Being so close to the humming ground sent the drone of their voices through my body until my teeth chattered from the vibration.

To the right of the parsonage, the huge maple tree began to shake. The ground around it lifted, exposing its massive root system. The shaking extended to the dirt under my own feet.

I began to quiver and I wanted to run but didn't know where to go, and was even more frightened that these terrifying women would see me.

The shaking grew ever more fierce and frightening until at last the maple crashed onto the front yard, its gnarled roots tipped skyward.

After the tree fell, the humming vibration ceased immediately.

The only sound was a rustling of treetops and the swish of blowing rye husks.

My chest ached from the pounding of my heart. What was going on? What had the ritual been about?

The strange women continued to stand there, observing the downed tree.

Now somewhat covered by the fallen maple, I stole back to the parsonage. What should I do next? Had the Parrises heard the tree go down? Should I tell them what I'd seen?

I didn't want them to arrest Bronwyn. Even if she was possessed of a demon, I couldn't risk having her executed or even jailed. How could I help her if that happened?

When I returned to the kitchen, it was aglow with the light from a small candle. It took me a moment to notice Tituba sitting on a stool in the corner, wrapped in an Indian-print blanket. In the dim illumination, I could tell more clearly from her broad features that she was not a native North American Indian but of a different sort, perhaps from the Caribbean.

We gazed at each other for a moment without speaking.

"I saw those demon witches from the window. Some terrible evil has come off that ship with you this day," Tituba said in a low, quiet voice. "And it has followed you here. Are you in league with this devilish thing?"

"No! You must believe me. No!" I recounted the entire story to her, starting with the wreck of the *Golden Explorer*. As strange as my story sounded to my own ears, Tituba showed no sign of disbelief. It was almost as if she had heard this sort of tale before.

"What do you think we should do?" I asked when I was done.

"Perhaps it will leave," Tituba suggested.

"And if it doesn't?"

"Magic is not all evil. There is powerful good magic too."

"I agree," I said, thinking of Aunty Honey in her role as Mother

Kadiatu, of Bronwyn before this thing took her over, and even of Saint Teresa of Avila. "I know there is good magic."

"Yes, I am now sure there is no evil in you. Good magic can defeat evil magic — sometimes."

"Should we tell Reverend Parris what we saw?" I asked. "He's a man of religion and holiness."

Tituba smirked bitterly. "He is a man of religion, but he has no holiness. Perhaps those demon hags have traveled here for his soul and not for you at all. I could believe that they have come for him."

"Then who should we tell? We have to warn the people of Salem that this evil haunts their village."

"Don't tell anyone. This village has been beset with many troubles. The farmers have suffered great crop failures. There have been epidemics of diphtheria and smallpox. The neighboring Indian tribes are angry with the treatment they have received, and attack the village regularly. There is much political fighting. Tempers are running hot. We don't want to enflame them. Who knows what would happen?"

"We can't stand here and let this evil run unchecked through this town," I insisted.

"We will watch for these evil witches. If they return, I know magic to dispel them."

I shook my head uncertainly, not convinced. "This is a demonic spirit of tremendous power," I told her. "It threw a priest over its head. It spun a huge ship in circles. It killed a nun and caused many of the people on board to fall ill. When I confronted it, the demon knocked me to the ground with its eyes alone."

Tituba remained unafraid. "My mother died and left me only one item," she said. "Her book of spells. I have it buried in the rye field and will consult it if the demons return."

Chapter Twenty

*A*T DAWN THE NEXT MORNING, I WENT TO THE WELL TO fetch water and saw Tituba's husband, John Indian, chopping the fallen tree into firewood. He didn't look up as I passed.

When I returned to the kitchen, Althea was playing with an adorable black child of about three. Althea smiled when she saw me. "This is Violet," she said. One look at the child's features told me Violet had to be Tituba's child, the resemblance was so great.

Setting down my full bucket, I shook the child's small hand. "Hello, Violet. I'm Betty. Where is your mommy right now?"

Violet pointed toward a closed interior door at the far end of the kitchen.

"Where does that lead?" I asked Althea.

"It's a dining room, but don't go there now," Althea warned. "Reverend Parris is talking to Tituba."

Reverend Parris's voice boomed from behind the door. "Do not lie to me, girl! I am warning you. I will not tolerate lies!"

Instantly, I was at the door listening.

"It is no lie, sir. I say once more — I could not sleep and was standing at the window gazing out. I saw four witches with a snarling demon dog. They employed magic to fell the large maple John now chops."

"Why would they choose my house for this witchcraft?" Reverend Parris pondered in an agitated voice.

My heart seemed to stop and I inhaled, awaiting Tituba's response. Would she tell him that the central witch had followed me off the ship and that all the witches had come for me?

"Because you are a man of God, sir," Tituba replied. "As such, you are the natural enemy of the Devil."

My heart began to beat again in my chest.

Soothed by Tituba's flattery, Reverend Parris's voice became less threatening but just as agitated. "Some discontented member of my congregation has set these witches on me. Maybe several have done it together. There is unrest amongst the flock. I am stern with them for the sake of their immortal souls and they have not the spiritual fortitude to hear it. Last month there was talk of ceasing to pay my salary or make their contribution to the upkeep of this parsonage."

"Surely those are wrongheaded decisions," Tituba said.

"Of course it is wrongheaded," Reverend Parris spoke passionately. "I will preach against it this Sunday from the pulpit."

The door banged open, pushing me behind as Reverend Parris barreled through, knocking over Althea and little Violet in his hurry. Violet began to wail and Tituba rushed in to lift and soothe her.

"Thank you for not mentioning me," I said.

Tituba nodded as she dried Violet's tears. "He's mean-spirited and you don't want to get on his bad side. The people in his church hate him. They would like nothing more than to be rid of him. He's not wrong to suspect them."

"I wonder what he'll say from the pulpit."

"This Sunday we'll find out," Tituba said as she set Violet back onto her feet.

"I can't go. I'm not a Puritan," I said.

Tituba shot me a sharp glance. "You are a Congregationalist Puritan now and do not forget it. It doesn't matter what you once were. You're a servant in a Puritan household and you will be expected to go to church this Sunday. We all will."

Later that same day, Tituba told me to ride in the carriage with John Indian and take a trip into Salem Town. He was hired out to work at a place called Ingersoll's Tavern for part of the day. I was sent with a purse of money to purchase food supplies.

Tituba held out a long brown cape. "This is mine; you can borrow it," she offered. "Take this bonnet too." She held out one of the simple white bonnets that tied under the chin. "You have to look proper when you are in town. Besides, it's very cold. I will make you a cape and bonnet of your own."

Along the way, I tried to make conversation with John Indian, but he kept his eyes straight ahead. We stopped in front of the tavern and he helped me out, telling me to meet him back there by four. When I asked, he directed me to the food market.

As I walked along the busy dirt streets, I kept a sharp eye for Bronwyn. I didn't know what I would do if I saw her, but I didn't want to be taken by surprise.

I also looked for Aakif. Hoping, even as hope felt foolish, that he was here somewhere. He had to be. But he never fell within my sight, no matter how hard I wished to see him.

The market bustled with activity and it was like a game to try to find the various items on Tituba's list, many of which — like dried cod, salt pork, turnips — I had never heard of before.

I was asking for a pound of dried peas when a hand clasped

my upper arm. Whirling toward it, I was reunited with Mary Carmen. We hugged, happy to see each other.

Mary Carmen was also dressed in the cape and bonnet of a Puritan. I was delighted to hear that her place of employment was not far down the road from the parsonage. We would be able to see each other and might even be able to coordinate our market days. It was at the home of a family named Putnam.

"Saint Teresa has appeared to me," Mary Carmen told me. Her dark eyes were bright with excitement. "She told me that Bronwyn is still on the astral plane trying to get through. The evil thing injured her, but she is still alive."

Mary Carmen dug through the pocket of her apron and pulled out a blue marble. "In my vision, Saint Teresa told me to meditate on this marble and it would calm my mind. It was in my hand when I came out of my trance."

"How amazing," I remarked, taking the marble from her. Reaching into the neckline of my dress, I drew out the blue glass bead that Aakif had given me. Since the day he'd put it on my neck, I had never taken it off. The blue of the glass marble and blue of the bead were exactly alike.

"Did she tell you anything more?" I asked.

"Saint Teresa said a great battle of the spirit is upon us, and that we will be called to act," Mary Carmen reported with quiet excitement.

I didn't like the sound of that — especially in the light of the previous night's events. I told Mary Carmen all about it and her face became pale with fear. She gripped my hand and squeezed. "These poor people," she said, looking around at the crowd. "This terrible evil has come to them and they don't even know it."

"They will know this Sunday," I said. "Reverend Parris is going to preach about it from the pulpit."

"Good," Mary Carmen said. "Then the people of Salem can band together to fight this wicked thing."

Chapter Twenty-one

"EVIL HAS COME TO SALEM!" REVEREND PARRIS'S VOICE boomed through his church. He pointed a finger at the congregants who sat in the pews facing him. I sat in the last row of pews beside Tituba, John Indian, and Althea. Everyone around me was a slave or a servant of some kind, so we were assigned the seats farthest from the pulpit.

"Salem shall burn with this evil just as Hell itself burns with the fire of Satan," Reverend Parris continued. He told everyone that he sensed some abomination had settled among them and that some in the congregation had summoned it through witchcraft.

Betty-Fatu!

I heard it in my head. Gazing around, I tried to locate the source.

Betty-Fatu! Look to your right.

The second time, I knew the voice. In another moment, I located Aakif sitting across the aisle from me in the last row of pews among other slaves and servants. He was trying to catch my eye by looking. His concentration was so intense that I'd been able to hear his thoughts.

Our eyes met and he beamed at me.

I met his smile with my own. He was also dressed as a Puritan, though his cape was patched and worn, his white collar frayed. How I longed to leave my seat and go wrap my arms around him. But just to see his dear, handsome face again would have to be enough for the moment.

Being prudent, we both diverted our gazes and faced forward. After a while, from the corner of my eye, I noticed him slowly rise and slip out of the pew. With the merest flicker of his eye, he signaled me to follow. And with a slight tip of my chin, I agreed.

After he had been gone several minutes, I slid from the pew and walked out into the cold, sunny day, searching for him. A pebble skidded past my feet and then another. I realized they were being thrown from a closely packed stand of birch trees several yards away.

It took all my composure not to run to him, but I walked as calmly as possible to the birches. Once we were in the enclosure of trees, I threw myself into his arms, covering Aakif's face with kiss after kiss. He held me tightly in his strong arms. Then we clung to each other, my head on his shoulder, each loving the warmth and comfort of the other.

"I am so happy you're here," I said after several more minutes. "It's a miracle that we've come to the same place."

"No miracle," Aakif disagreed. "I heard that they sent you here. When I learned they were also selling off some slaves to Salem, I asked to go so that I could find you."

"I thought you were going to be a foreman. You abandoned that chance. You shouldn't have done it, though I'm so happy that you did."

"They were happy to let me go. They said I was too soft on the workers and that I didn't know my 'place.' "

I squeezed him again, so deeply touched that he had come all this way to find me. And now we were together again.

"Listen to me, Betty-Fatu," Aakif said, stepping back from my embrace but still holding my shoulders. "Can you find a day to come to the shipyard in port?"

"On days when I do the marketing I can get there," I replied. "Why?"

"I've been bought by a family named Osborne who have a one-hundred-and-fifty-acre farm. They are not too bad as masters since Mr. Osborne came to this country as an indentured servant himself. When they discovered I could read and write, the Osbornes hired me out as a shipbuilder. They will allow me to keep some of my salary, which is more than I expected. I will be able to buy my freedom much faster than before."

"That's wonderful!" I cried. "How long?"

"I don't know yet. Sooner than it would have been if things were otherwise."

"It doesn't matter. I'll stay here and wait, no matter how long it takes."

"It won't be easy for us to be together," Aakif said seriously. "Everyone will be against it. In fact, it might be impossible. And it's too much to ask of you."

"We'll find a way. We'll go farm out in the country where no one else lives. We'll live on a boat in the middle of a lake."

He smiled at me. "You wouldn't mind that?"

"Not if I could be with you."

His smile was radiant; the most beautiful smile I had ever seen.

Aakif's expression grew serious as a new resolve overtook it. "When I'm free, we'll figure something out. There has to be somewhere in this big country where two people who love each other can be together." He gazed through the trees, worried. "I'd better get back. You too."

He walked back to the church, gesturing for me to wait before following.

Watching him go, I was once more overwhelmed by my love and admiration for him. My Aakif was here in Salem, close by. He had come all this way, gone through so much pain and humiliation to find me. My heart felt as though it would explode with joy.

And so the weeks rolled by, growing ever colder and grayer. As my best-loved holiday, Christmas, approached, I was disappointed to learn that the Puritans didn't celebrate it. They thought it was leftover from a non-Christian Roman celebration and wanted nothing to do with it.

Despite the austerity of their Puritan ways, life in the Parris family was bearable. Althea was a sweet roommate who loved word games and puns and was always lively. I warned her to stay away from the fortune-telling methods that Abigail was so drawn to. It would only lead to trouble for her, and she agreed.

Unfortunately, Abigail wasn't content to pursue the future on her own. She drew Betty Parris into her activities. One day I came upon them in the lean-to, holding a lit candle up to an egg. When I asked what they were doing, Abigail explained that the yolk of the egg showed pictures that foretold the future. Curious,

I gazed at the egg but saw nothing. I recalled that Mary Carmen had said St. Teresa had seen her vision of God's mansions in an egg, and that my own ancestors could predict the future. Just the same, I was fearful for their safety. "Mrs. Parris will be very upset if she sees you at this," I warned them. "For your own good, you should not do this."

"I'm not afraid of my aunt," Abigail replied scornfully.

Little Betty Parris didn't appear to be as confident but she nodded in agreement.

"Suit yourselves," I said as I took a bucket from a peg on the wall. "I've warned you." As I turned back toward the house, I was startled by a person who had crept upon me silently. It was the beggar woman Sarah Good, an unkempt, crouched woman with wiry gray hair.

It was said that she was not only poor and lacking a home but also mentally unstable. The wild look in her eyes made that claim believable. "Something to eat!" she demanded. "I need food."

I was about to offer to look in the kitchen when Abigail interrupted. "Go away, you hag!" she shouted. "Here's something for you!" She hurled an egg that splattered on the woman's ragged shawl.

Sarah Good raised a gnarled fist to Abigail. "I curse you, brat! You will regret this."

"*You* will regret coming here to bother us!" Abigail responded boldly.

The woman hobbled off, muttering curses under her breath. "I can find you something to eat," I called after her, but she paid no heed.

"Let her be off," Abigail scoffed.

"Did you have to be so cruel?" I scolded.

"She's disgusting," Abigail replied. "And I believe you are a servant and not allowed to speak to me in that tone."

I was not about to become embroiled in an argument with a spoiled girl, especially when she had a point — as a servant I was in no position to chastise her.

Despite Abigail's bold display, I knew that the confrontation with Sarah Good had rattled her. By the next day, Abigail had enlisted two older girls named Ann and Elizabeth to join in the egg experiment. By the following day there were five of them, all holding eggs up to candles with the intention of discovering the professions of their future husbands. If Sarah Good returned, she would find herself greatly outmatched.

Chapter Twenty-two

I COULD HARDLY WAIT FOR THE NEXT MARKET DAY, AND IT came on a Wednesday, two weeks later. As before, I rode in with John Indian, who said little. I huddled under the cape Tituba had made for me and was glad for my bonnet; the January day was bitterly frigid.

I met Mary Carmen at the market and learned that one of the girls who had been coming to join Abigail, Ann Putnam, Jr., was a member of the family she now served. "Those folks are too quarrelsome," Mary Carmen remarked. "It's so disagreeable to be among people who are always fighting not only amongst themselves but also with their neighbors, the Osbornes."

"That's where Aakif is," I told her. "What's their problem with the Osbornes?"

Mary Carmen told me that Mrs. Osborne's first husband had left the big farm to his two young sons. Mrs. Sarah Osborne was to be in charge of it only until her sons were old enough to claim their inheritance. But Sarah Osborne remarried the indentured servant on her property, Andrew Osborne, and wanted the will changed so she could inherit the property. John Putnam was her first husband's lawyer and was fighting her on it.

"I think John Putnam has influence over the Osborne sons and will be able to convince them to let him use their lands since it is right next to his own," Mary Carmen concluded. "I don't trust him."

I told Mary Carmen about Aakif being at the shipyard and bid her a farewell. Finding the shipyard wasn't difficult since I only needed to follow the sound of hammering to reach it. Hanging from the rigging of a ship in dry dock, Aakif saw me and called my name, waving. He swung down with nimble ease as though he'd been working on ships all his life, and met me on the gangplank. We walked back down into Salem Town together.

He loved the shipbuilding and felt he was learning a trade that could serve him well once he bought his freedom. I told him all that had happened with Bronwyn and her three witch companions, as well as the devilish dog.

"I hear talk of witches everywhere," Aakif remarked. He tapped his collarbone. "Do you have the bead I gave you?" I nodded that I did. "Then don't worry about bad juju. The bead will keep you safe."

"How can you be sure?" I challenged.

"I trust Aunty Honey. She was the one who gave it to me."

Back at the parsonage, I came in through the side entrance but stopped outside the door, clutching my bags of food. I noticed that someone had left the hatch of the root and grain cellar open. If it had been Tituba, she'd be sorely punished for such an oversight and I didn't want that to happen, so I set my bags down and went to shut it.

As I bent to shut the hatch, I gasped and jumped back. The gigantic black dog that had been with Bronwyn the other night growled at me from inside the cellar, his eyes burning.

I froze as the hound approached me, not knowing whether to run or stay still. At the top step, the hound leapt up at me.

Pulling myself into a ball, I waited to feel its horrific fangs sink into my flesh. But rather than attacking me, it sailed up over my head and disappeared.

Falling backward to the ground, my heart hammering, I was awash with terror and relief that resulted in a bath of hot tears in my eyes. Wiping them quickly, I sat a moment, looking down at the dark cellar before daring to venture into it.

Inside the cellar, everything had been torn apart. Sacks of

dried rye were spread across the floor. Barrels of potatoes were tipped. Jars of pickled vegetables lay smashed on the ground.

As I turned in a circle, looking at the damage, Abigail and her group of fortune-seeking girls appeared in the hatch doorway.

"What have you done?" Abigail asked in a taunting voice.

"I've done nothing. I found it this way," I defended myself.

"Oh, then it must have been Tituba."

"Not she, either. It was a very large dog that got in here. I saw it."

"My uncle always keeps this storage space locked. Did the dog have a key?" Abigail asked snidely.

"Of course not," I snapped.

"Then someone let him in or forgot to lock the door. I see that you have been entrusted with a key," she said, glancing at the ring of household keys at my waist.

"What have you come here for, Abigail?" I asked sharply.

"I need rye. We are baking dream cakes."

"What is a dream cake?" I asked.

"After we eat them, we will dream of our future husbands. That way each of us can recognize him when he comes along."

"What else is in these cakes?"

Abigail wiggled her fingers, mocking me. "Ohhhh, all sorts of spooky, witchy things — very secret ingredients." Her brows knit into a frown. "Let us have the rye or I will say you caused all this damage."

It seemed to me that I had no choice but to let them take the rye they wanted. I didn't think it would be missed anyway. "Where will you bake these cakes?" I asked.

"Over an open fire in the woods," Ann Putnam answered, showing the large frying pan she held.

After they'd loaded their pan with rye, the girls left. Only then did I notice the black specks scattered through the remaining kernels of tan rye on the floor. I'd seen rye at home and had never noticed anything like this. I gathered a handful of the grain and poured it into my apron pocket.

After bringing my packages into the kitchen, I took a broom and some rags out to clean the root and grain cellar as best I could. The cellar was always cold, and especially so on a January afternoon, so I worked quickly to accomplish my task and move inside as soon as possible. I was almost done when Tituba appeared in the doorway, her black hair undone and disheveled — clutching a carving knife. Her eyes were lit with a wild fire.

"Tituba! What happened?!" I cried as she collapsed into me, too weak to stand any longer.

"Witches!" Tituba sobbed.

I sat with Tituba in the kitchen and listened to her incredible story. She had been outside scrubbing the lean-to floor when the same three women we'd seen drop the large maple appeared out of nowhere and surrounded her. Bronwyn was inside their circle, accompanied by the black dog. Tituba swore the dog spoke to her in a growl, intoning the words: "Serve me!"

"I will not serve you," Tituba had insisted.

But then Bronwyn spoke. "We will cut off your head and return it to John Indian if you do not do as we say."

Tituba told me that the three witches kept spinning in a circle, chanting a spell while Bronwyn instructed her to torment Abigail and her friends with a large knife. When she refused once more, the three witches began shrieking their evil words at top volume and Bronwyn placed her hand on Tituba's head.

All at once, Tituba felt herself rise up and leave her own body.

"You were on the astral plane," I suggested breathlessly.

"I have heard of that and I think I was," Tituba agreed. "And so were the witches, for they had my spirit ride on a branch as they were. They were controlling the branch and so I was compelled to go with them. I saw no trees or path, but presently we were in the woods. There I saw Mistress Abigail Williams, Mistress Betty Parris, Mistresses Elizabeth Hubbard, Ann Putnam, and several other girls cooking some kind of cakes over an open fire in the forest. They used one of our frying pans."

"Was Althea with them?" I questioned, worried.

"No, Althea was not there."

"Thank goodness."

"The girls held hands and chanted words I did not recognize," Tituba continued. "As I watched them, some terrible evil took over my spirit. The evil you call Bronwyn directed one of her witches to take over my spirit. I was there but I was no longer controlling my own actions. I poked Abigail with my knife, causing her to cry out. As I did this, I reached out and pinched little Betty Parris on the arm."

"Could they see you?" I asked.

"I know they could because they faced me — or the entity that looked like me — as I slashed my knife back and forth. They begged me, 'Tituba, stop!' And, Betty, I longed to stop; I did everything in my power to control the movement of my knife-wielding arm, but I was helpless. Then two others appeared in spirit. One was Sarah Good, the other was Sarah Osborne."

"How did you know they were spirits?" I asked.

"Because they appeared from nowhere and I could see through them!"

"What did they do?"

Tituba shook her head forlornly and placed her hands over her eyes, as though she did not want to think about what had happened next. "The three of us tormented the girls, chasing them through the forest, kicking them, pulling their hair, jabbing them with sticks and my knife. But do you want to know something, Betty?"

"What?"

"I think those women were just like me. Something had entered them; the three witches were nowhere in sight during this. Your Bronwyn was doubled over, howling with vile laughter, but her minion witches were not near her as they usually are. I believe wholeheartedly that their evil spirits were inside of us women."

"How did you escape?"

"I don't know. Suddenly I was back at the lean-to, sprawled on the frozen ground, all alone."

"Are you positive it really happened?" I questioned. "Could it have been a dream?"

"I could have fallen sleep, I suppose. It seemed real, but when I tell it, the story sounds more like a dream." She rose from the table. "Let us go check on Abigail and little Betty. If they show signs of their torment in the forest, we will know."

Tituba and I ascended the stairs to the second floor, where the girls of the house shared a room. We were only halfway up the steps when we became aware of a commotion. Mrs. Parris was shouting, her baby was crying, and I heard loud barking.

"The black hound is back!" I cried, hurrying upward. But when I arrived in the bedroom, there was no black hound.

Little Betty was on all fours, growling at Reverend Parris as though she believed she was a dog. Just as I entered, she took hold of her father's pant leg and yanked on it as a dog might do, snarling all the while.

I immediately thought of the demonic black dog. Had its evil spirit entered little Betty?

"Betty, I'm warning you," Reverend Parris bellowed at his daughter. "There is no humor in this. Desist at once!"

Abigail was bouncing on the bed, waving her arms and laughing maniacally. A mad smile played across her face and she seemed not to realize anyone else was in the room.

Tituba came in behind me, amazed and distressed by what she saw.

Mrs. Parris held her baby, who was wailing. She looked to Tituba for help. "What is happening?" she implored. "Why are they acting this way?"

Tituba was too stunned to speak and probably wouldn't have known where to begin anyway.

Reverend Parris suddenly let out a howl of excruciating pain. Little Betty had sunk her teeth deep into his leg and would not let go. She seemed not to notice that blood covered her face as she dug her teeth into her father's flesh.

"Stop! Stop!" Reverend Parris shouted and flung his daughter across the room. Little Betty hit a wall but it didn't seem to bother her. She was immediately back on all fours, barking at all of us.

Thomas Parris ran in. "Oh, they're faking!" he cried indignantly. "Can't you tell? This is all a grand performance."

"Quiet, boy!" Reverend Parris demanded, stooping to wipe his bloody leg with a handkerchief. "The Devil's hand is in this!"

Abigail suddenly lost her crazy demeanor and let out a

deafening scream. "She's pinching me! She's pinching me! Make her stop!" With a robust bounce from the bed, she scrambled under a straight-back chair and once more broke into peals of hysterical laughter.

Reverend Parris rushed out and soon returned with a black book. "These words will exorcise the demons from them," he announced. He began to shout out passages from the book that exhorted the Devil to leave the premises, but it was to no avail. The girls did not cease their antics.

"What has happened to you girls?" Mrs. Parris pleaded. "Tell us! Please!"

Abigail came out from under the chair and stood, feet planted apart. "Tituba did this to us!" she shouted, pointing. "It's all her fault. She's a witch!"

All heads turned to stare at Tituba.

"I am no witch!" she defended herself.

Reverend Parris glowered at her. "You *are* a witch, Tituba," he accused in a towering voice.

"No. It isn't so!" Tituba insisted.

"It is!" Reverend Parris intoned. "And by the power of the clergy, you stand accused."

The next I knew, I was thundering down the stairs behind Tituba, sure I was the next to be accused.

Chapter Twenty-three

TITUBA SOUGHT REFUGE IN THE WOODS. "YOU MUST GO back," she urged me. "If you hide here with me, it will be the same as admitting you are a witch. Reverend Parris did not accuse you."

I knew she was right, and some time later I nervously returned to the parsonage. "Were you able to catch her?" Reverend Parris asked when I came in. He was sitting on a chair in the kitchen while Mrs. Parris attended to the bloody bite on his leg.

This question took me by surprise and left me speechless until I realized he'd misinterpreted my actions. He had thought that I was running after Tituba rather than fleeing right behind her.

"I did not, and I believe I was wrong to pursue her, sir," I said. "I do not believe that Tituba is a witch. Whatever delirium has seized the girls has caused them to believe things that are not so."

"Doctor Griggs has seen the girls," Mrs. Parris told me. "He can find nothing physically wrong with them and has concluded that their ravings have all the indications of bewitchment."

"If this is so, how can you be sure it is Tituba who is the witch?"

"Abigail named her. Betty seconded the accusation," Reverend Parris said. "They also named Sarah Good and Sarah Osborne."

I knew Abigail wasn't lying and neither was little Betty. They *had* seen Tituba in the woods, as well as the two Sarahs. The girls were telling the truth as best they understood it.

Several days later I met Tituba among the withered stalks of rye behind the parsonage. "My mother's book of spells is buried here," Tituba told me. "It is our only hope."

It wasn't easy to dig the cold winter ground, but Tituba and I banged at the hard earth, I with a hoe, and she with a shovel we took from the lean-to. We dug until a large patch of polished wood emerged from the dirt. Tituba tossed away her shovel and clawed the ground, pulling out the wooden box. When she pried it open, I saw a thick, worn leather book whose pages were so yellow and brittle I was afraid they would crumble and blow away if we dared to touch them.

Tituba opened to the middle section of the book. "We must banish this evil monster altogether — send it back where it came from."

"Is that possible?" I asked.

"Of course it is. People have been doing it since time began." She finally found what she'd been searching for. "Here it is!" A smear of dirt from her hands soiled the page but she paid it no attention. "These are the words the evil thing doesn't want to hear."

The passage was long and written in tiny handwriting, so I didn't bother to read it then. "It must be said along with the protection of powerful talismans," Tituba continued to read.

"What kind of talismans?"

"Objects to keep off the Devil and the evil eye."

I lifted the necklace Aakif had given me from under the neckline of my dress. Tituba smiled. "Yes, like that. I know that type from the isle of Barbados, where I lived for many years before coming here. It might be the thing we need."

Just then we heard boot steps crunching through the dead, fallen stalks of rye. Soldiers in gleaming breastplates and helmets approached us.

Tituba tossed the book of spells back in the hole and we both kicked dirt on it. I covered it with dead rye and then, on hands and knees, crawled into a thick patch of rye stalks. As the guards came closer, I lay flat on my stomach, face into the dirt, holding my breath.

Tituba was not as quick.

"Tituba the slave, you are under arrest," the lead soldier boomed. "You are charged with the crime of *maleficium*, witchcraft. You must come with us."

"I am no witch," Tituba objected.

"Just the same, you must come and be tried. You have been accused."

It was so hard not to look to the book of spells. If it were discovered so close to Tituba, it would not bode well. Fortunately, the guards were too busy shackling Tituba's wrists to notice it.

They marched her from the rye field and I lay flat and quiet a long time. Finally, when I felt certain they were gone, I got up and recovered the book of spells, and hurried off with it back into the parsonage.

Chapter Twenty-four

*I*T WAS THE MIDDLE OF MARCH AND I WAS AWAITING Aakif, who would, under the cover of darkness, meet me in the abandoned barn we had selected as our regular meeting place.

On March 1, when the judges questioned Tituba, she told them honestly what had happened. She had been ambushed by a terrible demonic force and kidnapped. Tituba *had* seen Sarah Good and Sarah Osborne there. When she tried to explain that these women, like herself, had been inhabited by evil spirits, no one credited it, or even understood what she meant. "There is a conspiracy of witches at work in Salem," she told them, speaking the absolute truth.

Tituba was still in jail, as were the two Sarahs. All were awaiting trial. But they were not alone. Every day, the jail was more and more crowded as Abigail, little Betty, Ann Putnam, Jr., Elizabeth Hubbard, a girl named Mercy Lewis, and others continued to have mad fits and accuse one person after another of bewitching them.

I didn't think they were lying, either — not for the most part, anyway. This demon that had invaded Salem was running havoc, having its attendant witches jump from body to body.

"These courtrooms are like carnivals," I said to Aakif when he arrived and sat on the floor of the barn beside me. "The girls claim evil spirits are right in the room with them. Every time one of the accused even moves a hand, they think they are under attack. They shake and quake and go into deep trances. I know the demon is responsible, but I wonder if there is some other cause as well. Maybe it's a sickness of some kind. I can't believe they're being bewitched at every second."

"I've been thinking of something, Betty-Fatu. Do you remember the cone grass Aunty Honey showed you how to use?"

I nodded, remembering it well.

"What if they're eating something like that and it's affecting them?"

"It's possible, I suppose. I don't know. They might still be eating those dream cakes. But the cakes are only just rye flour, butter, milk, and some sugar." Reaching into my apron pocket, I took out a few pieces of the black-specked rye that I had wrapped in a piece of cotton. I'd saved it to show Aakif.

Aakif inspected it. "What are those specks? The Osbornes' rye doesn't look like that."

"I don't know."

"I wonder," Aakif said. He picked up a few specks and smelled them. "It has no odor," he noted.

I dropped some on my tongue. "It's tasteless too."

Leaning back into Aakif's shoulder, I suddenly felt a powerful fatigue and drifted to sleep. How long I slept, I can't be sure, but I suddenly felt a sharp pinch on my arm and was instantly awake. Turning to Aakif to ask why he'd pinched me, I saw that he was sleeping soundly.

A low growl made me look abruptly to the source — and my heart turned to ice.

Scared, I clutched for the marble I always wore at my neck. It wasn't there.

Evil Bronwyn, her three attendant witches, and the black hound stood in a row staring at me.

"Serve me!"

The voice was definitely male and it had come from the dog.

A disturbing ring of numbness banded my arms and ran up and down the length of them. On the periphery of my vision, colored lights sparked, and I felt dizzy. Trying to rise, I fell backward.

"You've eaten the ergot rye," Evil Bronwyn said with a laugh. "You can't get away from us."

I suddenly felt as though an army of ants was crawling the length of my legs and was nipping at me as they went. Horrible! But were they real or only in my mind? Swatting at them, I discovered that they were indeed there.

Repulsed, I began to scream. "Stop it! Make them stop!"

"Serve me," the black dog growled again, his voice an unnerving rumble.

"No! No!" I shouted, quaking in fear yet determined not to submit to this horror.

My screams awoke Aakif. I could see and hear him but felt that he was too far away for me to reach. "Betty-Fatu," I heard him cry, "what's the matter?"

What was the point in answering him? He was so far away. So I turned back to the demonic crew. To my surprise, they had been joined by a sweet little child with bouncing blond curls. It was Dorcas Good. She began to sing and dance around me. "Little ants bite. They bite me and you. Little ants will eat Betty-Fatu!"

"How do you know I'm called Betty-Fatu?" I demanded, my voice quivering.

The little girl suddenly transformed into the slave master Parris. He lashed the ground beside me with his whip. "I know you, Betty-Fatu!" he growled menacingly. His form melted and he was once more a little girl singing about ants.

I covered my ears as the ants swarmed me.

"Serve me and I can make it stop!" the voice once more emanated from the black hound.

The ants were in my hair, crawling into my ears. I swatted at them, rolling and screaming.

Evil Bronwyn howled with laughter, clapping her hands with demonic glee. "Ah, the ergot rye is marvelous! It lets us in! It lets us in! And you can't get out."

I saw that three more women had entered the barn. I knew them from my trips into town. One was elderly Rebecca Nurse, and the others were her two sisters, Mary Easty and Sarah Cloyce. They stood where the three witches had been.

All three sisters seemed to be in a trance as they walked toward me. Frail and elderly as they were, they easily lifted my squirming, resistant body and carried it toward the black dog. The dog's face had taken on an oddly human and sinister expression.

"Serve me."

"Make the ants stop!" I implored. I was covered from head to toe with the maddening insects.

"Serve me and it will stop," the black dog spoke.

The sisters and Evil Bronwyn began to chant. "Serve him. Serve him. Serve him."

"Serve who?" I shouted. "Who am I serving?"

"You know who he is," Evil Bronwyn scolded. "You know his name."

Suddenly, two strong hands pulled at my stomach and I was lurched away from the sisters. Ice water was being thrown in my face and I was being shaken. Aakif's voice was shouting at me. "Wake up, Betty-Fatu! Wake up!"

I was in the barn and the first light of morning was filtering through. "Betty-Fatu, come back! Come back!" Aakif's voice was thick with urgency and he was waving something over me. It was the blue marble necklace. He had found it! He'd used it to dispel the evil spirits just as Aunty Honey had said it would.

Evil Bronwyn, her witches, the dog, the little girl, Rebecca Nurse, Mary Easty, and Sarah Cloyce were all gone. There was no sign of them, not even a footprint, as though they had never been there at all. "Was I having a nightmare?" I asked Aakif.

Aakif shook his head. "That was no dream. You were floating, Betty-Fatu! Floating in air! And look at your skin."

My arms, chest, and neck were scratched and clawed at. In some places, my skin bled. Even my cheeks were scratched.

"Were there ants crawling on me?" I asked.

"No, but you were acting as though you were covered with them."

He had seen nothing other than my frantic scratching and my body being lifted. He saw no one else in the room.

Suddenly faint, I slumped into Aakif's arms and he caught me. We settled down by the wall and, still lying in his arms, I told him all I'd experienced. "This is a lot like what those girls are saying," Aakif noted. "You say that Evil Bronwyn said that eating the rye is what lets them in. And we have this odd, speckled rye."

"This rye is in those dream cakes they're eating," I pointed out. I pulled the speckled rye seed from my apron pocket and thought of Van Leeuwenhoek. If he inspected this with his microscope, would he discover what they were?

"Van Leeuwenhoek's ship is still docked. We are repairing its rudder, which was greatly damaged," Aakif said, obviously having the same thoughts as I. "I haven't seen him leave on any other ship."

"Then maybe he is still at Harvard," I guessed hopefully. "Do you think perhaps you could get a sample of this rye to him and ask his opinion of it?"

Aakif nodded. "I am well thought of at the shipyard and not watched closely. I can say I need some replacement part from the Boston yard."

Pouring the rye into his hands, I nodded. "We should leave now. It would not be good to be found here together at daybreak."

Despite the danger, we sat for a while thinking about all that had happened. "I'm not doing enough," I said after a moment. "I have to tell them what I know."

"You will get yourself into trouble," Aakif warned.

"This is a demon, Aakif, and I brought it with us! We caused all this grief."

"You can't blame yourself," Aakif said, taking me in his arms. "How could you have known?"

"But I do know now. It's too powerful for me to fight, even with your help and Mary Carmen's. But maybe if I reveal what I know, the whole town together can fight it."

"Don't do it, Betty-Fatu. I beg you not to. The way things are in this town, it will come back to hurt you. You mustn't draw attention to yourself. You'll become a target."

"I have to," I insisted as I tied the cord with the necklace back around my neck.

"You'll be naming Mary Carmen and me. I'm still a slave. I have even less protection by law than the other people being accused."

"I won't name either of you."

Aakif threw his arms wide in exasperation. "I didn't come all this way just to see you hanging at the end of a gallows rope," he cried.

To stay silent any longer was not right. "I have to," I said.

Aakif walked with me back to the parsonage. "I have to go get Bronwyn back," I said to him. "I've waited much too long."

Chapter Twenty-five

THAT MORNING, I WAS WAITING FOR REVEREND PARRIS. HE went to the court every day and transcribed the testimony given. He brought the transcriptions home every night, which was how I knew all the details of the court procedures.

"Reverend Parris, I must talk to you."

He stopped and gave me his attention. I told him everything I knew.

"So you're saying that it was you who brought the demonic witches to Salem."

"It was not my intention, but yes."

"Come with me, please," Reverend Parris said calmly. He guided me toward the stairs and walked with me to my room. Althea was just finishing doing her hair and he ordered her to leave. "You will stay in this room, Mistress Betty, until I send the authorities to come for you."

"The authorities?"

"You have confessed to consorting with the Devil, have you not?"

"No!" I cried. "I've not consorted. I have been the victim of some great evil, just as everyone involved in these trials has been a victim. No one has willingly *consorted*. In her testimony, Tituba told the truth. It happened exactly as she has told you. And the rye in your storage cellar creates an altered state that so weakens anyone who eats it that the Devil may work its evil."

"*My* rye?" Reverend Parris's tone was scornful. "You are saying it is *I* who am to blame for this plague of witchcraft?"

"I'm not saying you intended it."

"How dare you attempt to sully my good name with such an accusation!" Reverend Parris shouted, his face red with fury. "I am a member of the clergy! I do not aid Satan's work!"

"I am not aiding it either! I am clear of any wrongdoing."

"It does not sound so to me. We will let the courts decide what to make of it." He shut the door and I heard the lock click. "My wife will not let you out under any circumstances, so don't bother making a fuss."

Pacing the tiny room, I cursed my own stupidity in believing
I could trust Samuel Parris.

I had to stop this. I had caused this mayhem — however unin-
tentionally — and it had to end.

I pulled Tituba's book of spells out from under my mattress,
where I'd hid it after she'd been arrested. The book was thick
and I didn't know how I'd find the spell Tituba had selected, but
when I came to the page with the streak of dirt from her hand,
I knew I'd gotten to the right place.

There was a knock on the door. "Betty, it's me, Althea. Are you
all right?"

"Althea, I need your help. Could you undo the outside bolt for
me? Reverend Parris has locked me in." Immediately the bolt slid
open and Althea appeared. I kissed the top of her head. "Althea,
you might hear that I'm a witch, but I'm not. I have to leave this
house right now and I may never come back, but I've loved sharing a room with you."

"Are you on the run?" she asked.

"In a way."

"Can I come? You might need help."

Her bravery and generosity touched me. "Not now, but I have
a feeling we'll meet again some day." Then I thought of something she could do and asked her to check if anyone was around.

"Just John Indian working in the yard," Althea reported when
she returned.

With Tituba's spell book gripped beneath my arm and Aunty Honey's jar of special honey in my hand, I sneaked down toward the kitchen. On the bottom floor, through the front windows, I saw two soldiers coming to arrest me. Keeping low, I was able to duck into the kitchen and out the door to the yard.

John Indian was chopping wood. He saw me run toward the rye field but kept on with his work. The rye had not yet sprouted but its stalks were high, providing good coverage. Bent low, I made my way through them until I could slip into the woods.

When I was deep among the trees, I stopped and sat cross-legged at the base of an extremely large pine. I breathed out slowly and then, even more slowly, I inhaled. I did this for almost ten minutes until my breath was deep and even. The energy in my body began to flow along my veins. Concentrating, I pushed that energy up along my spine until it circled in my forehead, filling my inner space with different shades of light. I gave myself over to the illumination in my head until there was no reality for me other than the swirling colors.

And then I was off, traveling the astral plane, zooming over landscapes, journeying through clouds, flying even higher into a place where it was all whiteness. I felt I was moving very swiftly, calling out to Bronwyn as I went.

She wouldn't answer.

Finally, I gave up. It was easy to forget time up here, and I couldn't afford to do that right now. With all my thoughts on returning to my body, I sped back down to it.

When I was grounded on earth once more, I knew the hard task before me. Terrified as I was, I had to move forward. I had to use my mind to contact a demon.

On my way toward Salem Town, John Indian came along in the wagon and told me to climb in. At first I said no, because I didn't want to get him into trouble. He scoffed at this. "My wife is imprisoned as a witch. You are her friend. Do you think I would not help you? Get in."

I climbed in, happy for the ride. He pushed a basket of food toward me. "I am bringing this to Tituba. Prisoners must arrange for their own food. Eat. There is plenty for her." Gratefully, I ate some corn bread, first clarifying that none of the stored rye had been used.

"The rye is tainted and is to blame for some of this," I told him. "Destroy what is left of it if you can."

"All of the rye?" he asked.

"Only the rye in the back part of the storage cellar. The girls who are making accusations have been making dream cakes out of it. I believe the rest of the rye, the rye in the kitchen, is all right. It doesn't have those black specks in it."

He nodded in his taciturn way.

In Salem Town, he left me off, wishing me well. I made my way to the market and Mary Carmen saw me before I found her. I pulled her off to a side alley, not wanting to be seen or to have anyone notice Mary Carmen speaking to me.

I told her that I had been accused.

"It's going to be all right. Saint Teresa of Avila came to me again last night, Betty-Fatu," Mary Carmen said excitedly. "She will help us in our battle against the Devil, but she says we must be very brave. It won't be easy."

I was stunned that Mary Carmen had this to say — how had she known?

"That's exactly what we must do," I told her. "It's what I came to tell you. No one else will believe what's really happening."

Mary Carmen took a narrow vial of water from her apron pocket. "It's holy water," she told me. "I have carried it with me from Barcelona and have kept it for years. I think now might be the time to use it."

"Keep it close," I said, "and also the blue marble from Saint Teresa. We're going to need all the help we can get. Somehow, we will figure out a way to defeat this thing."

I left her then and went to find Aakif at the shipyard. As usual when he spied me, he came off the ship's rigging.

"Let's not talk here," I warned.

"I have been accused," I told him once we stood together at the shaded end of the alley, away from the street.

Immediately, he wrapped his arms around me. "We'll go away," he said. "Tonight, I won't go back to the Osbornes' but I'll meet you at the barn. We'll leave before they find you."

"No. We have to fight this thing," I objected.

"You are brave, Betty-Fatu; but how? Do you really think that we can take on the Devil?"

"Maybe it's not the Devil," I suggested, "but only some evil force."

"What does it matter? You've seen what it can do. Pride is a sin too, you know. Pride can destroy a person. Don't let it destroy you."

What he said made sense. I didn't even know how to find these witches and their hideous, terrifying black hound.

"All right," I agreed. "But we have to bring Mary Carmen with us. I can't leave her behind."

"Fine. Surely. We will meet tonight at the barn and then go to the Osbornes' together to get her."

"Did you see Van Leeuwenhoek?"

Aakif nodded. "I just returned minutes ago. He was intrigued and looked at the specks while I was still there. He said to tell you there are animalcules in the rye. His colleagues there said it was a mold called ergot."

I recalled the evil Bronwyn referring to this as ergot rye.

"When eaten, ergot rye makes symptoms such as the girls display: muscle twitching, nausea, jerking limbs, and delirium. It can kill a person," Aakif continued.

"This is amazing, Aakif. It must be what allows the evil creatures into the mind of their victims," I realized. "We have to get them to stop eating those dream cakes."

"Forget it, Betty-Fatu. Let's just get you away from here where you'll be safe."

"I don't know. I have to think on it. It doesn't seem right to run."

"Van Leeuwenhoek is going to write to Governor Phips. He will tell him what he's learned."

Two guards walked by and one of them glanced at us. My heart nearly stopped but they kept going. "I have to get back into the forest where it's safe," I insisted. "If they catch us together they will arrest you, as well as me."

"I will risk that," Aakif told me as we walked back toward the street. "Nine o'clock tonight at the barn. Bring everything you have that you will want to take with you."

Aakif left first, and a few minutes later I emerged from the alley. It was too early for John Indian to be done with his work at the tavern, so I set out on foot, my face averted from the passersby, out of Salem Town and back toward Salem Village where I knew the forest well.

My mind raced with the possibilities before me. What good would I be to anyone if I was incarcerated in a cell like Tituba, Sarah Good, and Sarah Osborne? But something deep inside told me that to run away and save only myself was wrong. I knew Aakif was thinking only of me, and I loved that he cared so much. I just didn't know what I should do.

With my head down, I passed through the streets, almost forgetting where I was. But suddenly I started and cried out in shock. Hands gripped both my arms. There were guards on either side of me.

"Elsabeth James, you are under arrest. You have been charged with *maleficium*. Witchcraft."

Chapter Twenty-six

ON THE DAY OF MY TRIAL, MARCH 19, GUARDS BROUGHT me to the courtroom just as Rebecca Nurse was giving testimony.

A black-robed judge in a white wig sat at a high desk. I saw Althea among the people who'd come to witness the trial. She smiled at me, but I didn't want to acknowledge her for fear of involving her in any way.

Among the spectators, I was surprised to see the native Indian father and daughter, the same pair who had come to Salem with us on the ship. There were many others whom I knew.

At a table to the judge's right, Reverend Parris sat behind an open ledger, quickly recording everything that was being said. In the front row, to my left, sat Rebecca Nurse's sisters, Mary Easty and Sarah Cloyce.

As I walked in, they looked sharply in my direction. I was sure they recognized me from the night in the barn. I longed to tell them it had not been me who'd accused them. Four-year-old Dorcas Good sat off to the side with her mother, looking pale and sickly, with dark circles under her eyes. How I pitied the little girl.

On my right sat the accusing girls. They also appeared frayed and exhausted by this ordeal, their hair tangled and dirty, skin blemished, their eyes wild and sunken. It was not surprising to me, knowing as I did that they had been in a drugged delirium for weeks.

Abigail Williams suddenly jumped from her spot and threw her hands in the air. "She's twisting my neck!" she shrieked, pointing at poor, elderly Rebecca Nurse with one hand and clutching her neck with the other.

An icy draft hit me when I walked near the bench where the accusers sat. I was certain that Evil Bronwyn, the three witches, and the black hound were present. I aimed my mind-reading ability in their direction. Murmuring and mumbling filled my head, as did wild, shrieking laughter. *We see you, Betty-Fatu! There's a speck of ergot still in your pocket. Taste it and join us!*

Reaching into my apron pocket, I discovered that there was, indeed, a black speck still there, clinging to the fabric. Now I was certain that the evil forces were right here with us.

The guards bid me to sit on the bench beside the other accused.

A tall, stern-looking man in his fifties had been interrogating Rebecca Nurse. Now he turned to Abigail. "Goodwife Nurse is all the way over here," he pointed out, even as Abigail still clutched at her own neck. "How could she be afflicting you?"

"Her spirit afflicts me," Abigail insisted. "Her specter is beside me."

"I see it!" shouted Ann Putnam. "She is with her sisters and she torments us."

"No!" Mary Easty objected as Ann collapsed, trembling from head to toe, her black boots banging on the floor, her back and head seizing as though she was being throttled.

John Hathorne, the judge, turned to Rebecca Nurse. "Goody Nurse, here are two — Ann Putnam and Abigail Williams — who complain of your hurting them. What do you say to it?"

"I can say before my eternal Father, I am innocent and God will clear my innocency. I am innocent and clear. I have been ill and unable to leave my house for the last eight or nine months."

As much as I believed she was telling the truth, I too had seen her at the barn that night, along with her sisters and Dorcas.

"Are you innocent of this witchcraft?" John Hathorne pressed her.

Exasperated and exhausted, Rebecca Nurse dropped her head and spread out her hands in despair. "Oh, Lord, help me!" she cried.

The girls on the front bench shrieked in pain, twisting in agony. "She tortures us!" Mercy Lewis cried out. "Her hands. Make her put down her hands."

"No, I will not sign it!" Abigail Williams shouted, talking to some invisible entity. "It is the Devil's Book! I will not sign it."

Hathorne whirled on Rebecca Nurse. "You would do well if you are guilty to confess and give glory to God!" he bellowed. "Is it not an accountable case that when you are examined, these persons are afflicted?"

"I have nobody to look to but God," Rebecca Nurse answered passionately.

"Do you believe these afflicted persons are bewitched?" John Hathorne questioned in a thunderous voice.

"I do think they are," Rebecca Nurse answered. In fact, she knew they were. Like Tituba, she had memory of the event but no way to stop it. I knew she was not telling all that had happened, knowing that the truth would be twisted.

John Hathorne pointed at the hysterical, twitching girls. "What do you think of this?" he demanded.

Exasperated, Rebecca Nurse shouted her answer. "I cannot help it; the Devil may appear in my shape!"

When they brought me up to testify, I told my story as accurately as I could. "And so you see, I am sure there is evil afoot in Salem and the rye these girls are eating is infested with a substance called ergot that allows these evil forces to afflict them."

Mercy Lewis was instantly on her feet. "It's a lie! We have done no wrong. We have not attempted to tell fortunes, nor have we made these dream cakes she speaks of."

"It's you who lie," I shot back. "You know you have eaten them."

Elizabeth Hubbard, a girl of seventeen, who was a maid in Dr. Griggs's household and one of the accusers, also jumped up. "You hope to shift your guilt to us with this lie. You are an evil witch."

All the girls nodded and murmured their consent. Only little Betty Parris averted her eyes guiltily.

"Tell the court again how you survived the shipwreck of the *Golden Explorer*," John Hathorne bid me.

"I swam until I found a barrel to float in."

"You swam?"

"Yes."

"Who taught you to swim?"

"My governess, a good woman named Bronwyn."

"This same Bronwyn who you claim has been taken over by the Devil?"

"Yes, taken over through no fault of her own."

"And this Bronwyn guided you . . . coming to you as a witch flying through the night . . . to the Isle of Devils where you were instructed in spells and potions by an African Witch?"

"No!" I objected. "They are good women. Healers!"

"Everyone knows that the ability to swim is a sign of a witch!" John Hathorne shouted at me. "Everyone here knows it. You were taught to swim by a witch and are, yourself, also a witch!"

"No!"

"You are the granddaughter and great-granddaughter of witches who have been put to death for their compliance with the Devil in practicing witchcraft. You are from a familial line of the Devil's handmaidens!"

His accusation left me speechless. What could I say to it?

John Hathorne grinned at me in smug triumph. "I have researched your family tree, Elsabeth James. The secret of your devilish family has been revealed. What say you to it?"

"They were not witches and neither am I," I replied quietly.

"You claim you have seen this Bronwyn the witch and her three witch helpers. You have seen the snarling Hound of Hell. I say you are the Devil's Consort."

"She is friend to Tituba who set upon us in the woods!" Ann Putnam, Jr., shouted.

"And when I told the witch Sarah Good to leave the property, Elsabeth James scolded me," Abigail put in with a vengeful and satisfied glance at me.

The judge banged his desk impatiently. "I have heard enough. Elsabeth James, I find you guilty of witchcraft. You will await your sentencing in jail!"

Chapter Twenty-seven

*I*N THE NEXT MONTHS, THE DEMONIC PRESENCE RAN RAMPANT through Salem, causing chaos and misery at every turn. The village was engulfed in a frenzy of accusation and counteraccusation. In April, Rebecca Nurse was convicted of witchcraft. When her sisters testified for her, they too were convicted. All were condemned to hang.

A woman named Elizabeth Proctor was accused by her servant Mary Warren. When her husband, John, protested, he too was convicted of witchcraft. Mary Warren said she had lied, then took it back, saying she had not lied. It was madness.

In the first week, Mary Carmen came with food for me. Up until then, Tituba had been sharing the food John Indian brought for her. For comfort, I also dipped into Aunty Honey's jar of honey. It was still edible, since honey never spoils, and I discovered that nothing made me feel stronger or calmer.

"Aakif will come soon," Mary Carmen told me. "Mr. Osborne will send food with him for his wife. He has written to Van Leeuwenhoek at Harvard."

"Do you think he will be of any help?"

"I hope so. Perhaps Van Leeuwenhoek can convince the governor to stop this madness. He is a renowned figure and has influence."

My only relief was that Aakif did, indeed, begin to come to the cell every other day to bring food to Sarah Osborne. Afterward, he sat with me and we talked. I told him of the effects of the honey and he wasn't surprised. "Keep eating it. It has great power," he said. We thought it might be unsafe to show our love too openly, but the brush of his hand over mine or a secret caress of my back gave me more comfort than I can say.

In May, Sarah Osborne grew ill, but despite her fever, they would not take off her shackles. Aakif came to bring her a basket of food and discovered her condition. "Bring my husband," she requested.

Aakif seemed reluctant to leave her, but I said I would look after her. I made a drink from the special honey that Aunty Honey had given me. Tituba gave me some of the cider John Indian had brought her that was mixed with chamomile and ground birch bark.

"Bless you both," Sarah Osborne said as I put the tonic to her lips. "You know I am no witch."

"Forgive me for naming you," Tituba implored. "I saw you in the woods that day, as you saw me. I know you were not acting on your own accord. I am so sorry. I believed they would understand me if I told the truth of what happened. I see now I was naïve."

"Evil is afoot here," Sarah Osborne said. "Demonic evil and human evil. It is true that my body was spirited away by some devilish force. And it is also true that John Putnam hates me because I have tried to claim what was rightfully mine. My dead husband and I bought and worked that farm together. It should have been left to me. Putnam hates that a woman should challenge the law. I never had a chance of being understood. What has happened to me is not your fault, Tituba. There is nothing to forgive."

I knew that the birch bark would soothe her pain and the chamomile would let her rest. Both were mild medicines, but they seemed to help.

Later, Aakif returned with Andrew Osborne. Sarah Osborne was able to speak to her husband for a long time before the guards made him leave. Andrew Osborne had summoned Dr. Griggs but he had refused to come.

In the morning, Sarah Osborne — still shackled — was dead.

In June, a person named Bridget Bishop was the first woman hanged as a witch. I knew her from jail and believe they hanged her more for her irreverent comments and colorful dress than anything else. When I asked her if she'd had any experience with the demons I'd met, she didn't know what I was talking about.

In July, five women, including Sarah Good and Rebecca Nurse, were hanged on Gallows Hill. In August, four men and one woman were hanged. Elizabeth Proctor was convicted but not hanged because she was pregnant. But her husband, John, was one of the five killed. On the day her husband died, Elizabeth wept loudly the entire time. Although it was awful to listen to, no one asked her to stop.

Also, in September, a man named Giles Corey, who had been accused back in April, was crushed to death under the weight of huge stones. As I sat in my prison cell, I felt a terrible pressure on my chest and grew breathless just thinking about it.

"I will lose my mind in here," I confided to Aakif.

"I bring you books, but the guards won't let them in," he replied.

I squeezed his arm tenderly. "I understand. If it wasn't for you and Mary Carmen, I would already be raving mad."

"Be strong, Betty-Fatu. We will find a way out of this. There are people in town who have written a petition to stop these trials. Mary Carmen has set up a prayer meeting of people who want this to end."

"How many people have joined her?" I asked.

"Many, and more are coming every hour. They sit in a field and chant short prayers over and over, asking for help against this evil that has beset Salem. In one hand, she holds a blue marble, and in the other, a vial of water. They have been doing it all day and it's still going on."

That night I could not sleep. My sentencing would be in the morning. As I twisted on my patch of straw, I heard a voice. Lifting my head to see if one of the other prisoners was talking, I heard only light snores.

But the voice came again. *"It's me, pet."* Sitting immediately, I saw Bronwyn beside me.

Thinking it was a visitation from Evil Bronwyn, I jumped up, but one look at her familiar soft eyes told me it was Good Bronwyn. In the next second I clapped my hand to my mouth in stunned surprise, the emotions of joy and relief whirling together.

"That awful thing kept me stuck on the astral plane with its spells. But today something has changed. The entity is being weakened by something."

Was Mary Carmen's prayer group having some effect on the evil creatures? It had to be.

"What should I do, Bronwyn?" I asked.

"You must join me on the astral plane. We have to move now while the creature remains weak."

"I don't have the strength to rise from my body. I'm sorry, but I don't feel I can." The months in prison had been so difficult. Not only my body but my spirit had been weakened.

Bronwyn surveyed me critically. "You are dispirited. I can see that."

"Let me eat some of this," I suggested, opening my jar containing the last of the honey. When I felt restored by its power, I told Bronwyn I was ready. "But I'm not sure I remember how."

"Remember what I've taught you. Sit cross-legged and focus your breath. Let the spirit rise along the length of your spine. As it rises, stabilize the vibration. Concentrate on not dropping back down."

I did as she said, and with a flash of white light, we were both hovering above the prison. Good Bronwyn beckoned and I followed her until we were over the shipyard. She gestured below and I saw Evil Bronwyn writhing in pain on the deck of a large ship.

"Why is it on a ship?" I asked.

"It is trying to get as far as possible from the source of its irritation."

Good Bronwyn and I came up with a plan. In our astral forms, we traveled to Aakif. He was asleep in the hayloft where the

Osbornes had created a room for him. I set down beside him and whispered in his ear until he began to awake. Suddenly he sat upward. "Betty-Fatu! Are you a ghost?" He jumped to standing. "Have they killed you?" He clutched his stomach. "Tell me it isn't so!"

"No! No! Don't be afraid, sweet. I'm traveling in spirit. Now you must listen to me, please." I told him to go to Mary Carmen. "Tell her group to keep praying no matter what." Then I asked him to go to the prison and bring my bag to the shipyard.

"Won't they realize you're gone if I do that?" he asked.

"No. My body is still there. They will think I am asleep." I gazed at his dear, handsome face. "I will do everything to get back to you," I said. "And if I don't, know that I will love you for all time, even if I die."

"Don't say that! You won't die. You can't die."

"The good Bronwyn is here with me. I'm not alone."

I kissed him, and though he couldn't see me, he stood still and his eyes took on a happy gleam. "You *are* alive," he said quietly.

Chapter Twenty-eight

*B*RONWYN AND I LOWERED OURSELVES CLOSER TO THE SHIP. We stayed above deck, though, and once more hovered over the writhing figure of Evil Bronwyn. A familiar low growl immediately filled the air. The black hound's yellow eyes blazed. Its fangs were bared. Good Bronwyn and I grabbed for each other's hand.

Cautiously, with our eyes on the snarling dog, Good Bronwyn and I approached the thing that had taken over her form.

"I do look the worse for wear," Bronwyn commented wryly.

"You've looked better," I agreed. "How can we fight this thing, Bronwyn? Is it possible?"

"If you give in to fear, we can't win," she said, giving my hand a reassuring squeeze. "I met one of your friends while I was on the astral plane. I have contacted her."

"Who?" I asked, but before I could answer, sparks like a meteor shower crossed the sky. Aunty Honey — dressed regally as Mother Kadiatu — was suddenly hovering beside me. The sight of my old teacher nearly brought tears of happiness to my eyes. I knew how powerful her magic would be.

"I have the potent magic from my home in Sierra Leone, the secret words to banish the bad juju," Mother Kadiatu said.

"And I have the women's words from my village, the ones that will banish a devil," Bronwyn assured me.

"Hold tight to the talisman Aakif gave to you, Betty-Fatu. Whatever happens, don't let the demon take it from you," Mother Kadiatu insisted. "You are a strong girl who floated the wide ocean in a barrel. Remember who you are."

The black dog growled at us, and made Evil Bronwyn aware of our presence. Evil Bronwyn sat up, glaring intensely at us with a look of pure hatred. Though we were on the astral plane, it could tell we were there.

I clutched the bead at my neck as Mother Kadiatu began chanting words of goodness and words of power in her native tongue. Good Bronwyn spoke words of magic in her ancient Scottish.

Evil Bronwyn gripped its ears, cringing. Doubling over in pain, purple-black clouds rose around it. Evil Bronwyn's skull cracked open from the forehead to the base of its skull. Bronwyn's body fell like a robe as a hideous fiend of immense height, with veined skin of deep purple, emerged, reminding me of a skinned animal. It spread immense wings of the same purple, beating the air in a triumphant gesture.

Now it was able to see us hovering above. Staring up, it let out a scream so high-pitched it seared through me like a flame. I saw that the black dog had fallen to the ground, unconscious. "Serve me!" the evil creature bellowed. "Serve me!"

With a wide sweep of its arm, the demon pulled me down into its crushing grip. Good Bronwyn and Mother Kadiatu threw themselves onto its arm, but they were helpless against it.

"Serve me!" it screamed into my face.

Aakif ran up the gangplank, my bag in hand. "Betty-Fatu?" he called, looking around frantically for me. He could not see any of us.

He took Tituba's book of spells from the bag. "I have your book," he shouted, sensing the tumult in the air.

I wanted to call to him but the demon was holding me in its crushing grip. Mother Kadiatu and Good Bronwyn came down beside Aakif. Mother Kadiatu took the book from his hands. "What page?" she shouted.

"Dirt" was all I could manage to reply, but she understood and found it quickly. Mother Kadiatu handed it to Aakif, though to him it seemed to float into his hands.

He understood and began to read the words.

The demon shook me and jostled the blue bead from beneath my collar. At the sight of it, the demon recoiled, but didn't drop me.

Mother Kadiatu and Good Bronwyn resumed their chant. Aakif read from Tituba's book of spells in a loud, impassioned voice.

The demon threw me to the ship's floor and strode toward Aakif, its eyes glowering. Rising to my feet, I ran to Aakif's side. This creature could not get hold of him.

Suddenly, the demon fell to its knees, clutching at its head. Down on the road, lights were glowing as wagons filled with praying people pulled up beside the shipyard. The lights were from lanterns and candles, and I could hear the people chanting over and over in a group voice that reverberated through the air: "Lead us not into temptation but deliver us from evil; lead us not into temptation but deliver us from evil."

Mary Carmen ran up the gangplank just as the demon knocked Aakif down with one powerful swat of its hand. She seemed to know what was happening and — while still saying the end of the Lord's Prayer — she poured a circle of the holy water around Aakif.

The demon could not cross the circle and, shrieking in rage, turned on Mary Carmen.

"Run, Mary Carmen!" I shouted, momentarily forgetting that she couldn't hear me on the astral plane.

Then I saw that Mary Carmen was not alone. Hovering above her on the astral plane was a beautiful woman dressed in a nun's habit. It had to be Teresa of Avila.

Saint Teresa locked eyes with the demon and then threw her hands to the heavens, shouting words I didn't understand.

VEHUIAH

JELIEL

SITAEL

ELEMIAH

MAHASIAH

LELAHEL

The astral plane flashed with light as one by one, tall, winged, glowing angels appeared. Their light was so blinding that the demon covered its eyes.

My ears filled with a vibrating hum that seemed to come from the angels and mixed with the prayers. "Lead us not into temptation but deliver us from evil. . . ."

Saint Teresa continued:

HAHAIAH

MEBAHEL

NELCHAEL

YERATEL

MANAKEL

HAZIEL

Her voice rose even louder, awe-filled and magnificent. "I call down the seventy-two angels by their names as written in the mystic book of Kabbalah."

A heavenly host of the most beautiful creatures I have ever witnessed appeared. When the last, the one she named Haziel, came, he stepped forward holding a shining sword. Before the demon could react, the angel Haziel swept the demon above his head and flung him into the sky. Images of the three attendant witches flew up in its wake, as though they were a part of the demon's body.

The majestic angels blinked away in the same order they had appeared.

Mary Carmen ran back to the gangplank and waved her arms to the praying people. "The evil has been defeated!" she shouted to them.

My heart burst with ecstatic happiness — but it was brief.

Bronwyn's body lay sprawled on the deck of the ship, lifeless. A deep gash bled where the demon had split her skull.

Good Bronwyn looked down on her ruined body. "I don't want to live up here on the astral plane," she murmured. "I've been here too long already."

Mary Carmen rushed to the supine body and placed her hands on Bronwyn's skull. With a soft blue light radiating from her palms, she held tight to Bronwyn. The bleeding stopped, but the body didn't stir.

Without speaking, Mother Kadiatu, Good Bronwyn, and Saint Teresa held hands. I joined them too. I saw an energy flowing across the four of us. It was a deep blue.

Below us, Mary Carmen raised her left arm and, like lightning is attracted to a tree, our energy jumped to her hand in an azure stream. The blue suffused Mary Carmen and passed out of her right hand into Bronwyn's body.

Bronwyn's eyes opened wide and then shut again.

Exhausted, Mary Carmen wilted to the ship's deck.

Off in the distance, I heard the steady beat of a drum.

Chapter Twenty-nine

*D*AWN LIGHT FILLED MY PRISON CELL AS I AWOKE, BACK IN my body. "Don't let it have been a dream," I whispered. It had been so real, and yet I couldn't be absolutely certain. Glancing to the corner where I kept my jar of honey and other supplies, my heart sank when I saw that it was still there. How did it get from the ship back into my cell?

"Thank the heavens." Turning toward the voice, I saw Tituba sitting beside me. "You have been unconscious for two days," she told me.

"Two days?"

"Yes, my friend, two days. You have had visitors too."

I sat up. "Who?"

"Aakif and Mary Carmen."

"Did they bring my bag?" I asked excitedly.

"Yes, we brought it!" Aakif said from the doorway. Before I could rise, he was at my side and we were hugging each other tightly. Mary Carmen was right behind him and we too embraced.

"You will never believe who we've seen!" Aakif said.

"Van Leeuwenhoek heard what was happening in town and came to talk to Reverend Parris. We heard he was at the parsonage and sought him out early this morning," Mary Carmen revealed.

"And Governor Phips has moved to terminate the trials," Aakif went on. "It seems that someone has charged the governor's own wife as a witch!"

"Everyone is free?" I asked as Mr. Van Leeuwenhoek entered the cell.

"I'm afraid not," Van Leeuwenhoek said. "No one can leave until they pay for their board in this horrible place. I find that unbelievable. But you are free. I have paid your way out of this horror."

"You are too kind to me, but I thank you with all my heart," I told him sincerely.

"It is my pleasure to help such a brave young woman," Van Leeuwenhoek replied.

Turning to Tituba, I smiled. "We can go," I told her. "As soon as Reverend Parris pays your board, you can leave. You'll be back with Violet and John Indian."

Tituba shook her head unhappily. "John was here this morning. Samuel Parris will not pay. He thinks I've disgraced his family by speaking the truth. John has not the money, either. Parris says whoever wants to buy me as a slave is welcome and must also pay to get me out of here."

"I will pay," Van Leeuwenhoek offered.

"Thank you, sir. You will find me a hardworking slave," Tituba said emotionally.

"You will not be my slave," Van Leeuwenhoek answered.

Tituba gasped with delight. "It is too much to ask!" she cried.

"Not at all," he answered, with a gracious bow.

For the first time in months, I was out in the sunshine in front of the prison. Van Leeuwenhoek, Mary Carmen, and Aakif were beside me.

Looking debilitated and stooped, several more women left the prison, squinting against the bright light, surrounded by their families. They came in small groups, not jubilant, but weary and eager to get home.

Tituba had returned to the parsonage to collect her things and rejoin her family. They all assured me that what occurred the night before had been no dream. Bronwyn was resting in Aakif's room at the Osborne home.

"I have news," Aakif said.

"What?" I asked. "Is it good or bad news?"

"Excellent news."

"Tell us," Van Leeuwenhoek prodded.

"Andrew Osborne lowered the price for my freedom," Aakif reported. "He knows what it is to be a slave. I had enough to buy my freedom, and in fact, I paid him this morning. I am a free man."

I gasped and we stared at each other, not quite believing it. "You did it," I whispered.

He nodded as his expression changed from one of disbelief to that of glowing happiness.

"You did it!" I shouted as he swept me into his arms and spun me in a circle. When we stopped spinning, I held on to him so tightly. He was free! I was free! There were tears in both our eyes.

"It is a great day, indeed!" Mary Carmen cried happily.

When we finally settled down, Van Leeuwenhoek had a question, which he addressed to Mary Carmen. Though we'd told him all that had happened, he was still puzzled on one point. "Isn't Saint Teresa of Avila considered a Catholic mystic?"

"She is," Mary Carmen confirmed.

"Then how did she come to call on the seventy-two angels by name? You said she named something called the Kabbalah, a Jewish book, as her source."

"Saint Teresa's grandfather was Jewish, but forced to convert to Catholicism by the Spanish Inquisition. But Saint Teresa's father and grandfather studied the mystic Kabbalah in secret. They allowed her to study it also," Mary Carmen explained.

"What shall we do now?" I asked. I certainly was not going back to that parsonage — not ever. And what was left for me now in England with Kate and Father gone?

Before anyone could answer my question, the young Indian native who had been with her father on the ship to Salem approached our group. "Greetings," she said, speaking to me. "I am Winun'na. We have seen each other but we have never been introduced."

"Hello, Winun'na. I am called Betty-Fatu. I am pleased to meet you," I replied. I introduced Van Leeuwenhoek, Aakif, and Mary Carmen. "I remember you well. I saw you and your father at my trial," I added.

Winun'na nodded gravely. "It is a bad business. My father is the holy medicine man of our tribe, which you whites call the Massachuset. As a shaman, he knows that the whites think we worship Matchitehew — the evil one. We do not, of course — but it helps him feel the sorrow of what you are going through. It is true pain to be so misunderstood."

"That is kind of you to say," I replied.

"My father is greatly distressed by what has happened here and has been imploring the Great Spirit to aid you. Last night, he sensed a great war between good and evil was being waged. He banged the drum and sang to the Great Spirit all the night through. He sent me here this day to offer his help."

I took her hand as I spoke. "Something very great has occurred. Tell him we thank him greatly for his help. Last night, a terrible evil was driven away and I am sure — certain — that his chanting and drumming enabled us to succeed."

Winun'na shut her eyes, genuinely moved. "It will mean so much to him." I told her too that the prison was being opened and the trials disbanded.

"The people of my village are disbanding as well," Winun'na revealed. "It is getting too crowded since we have been pushed off much of our land. Some of us younger Massachuset are heading north, to a territory on the shore of the very large Lake of Shining Waters. The Huron and Iroquois People are there now but there is much land and we think we can peacefully make a place for ourselves. We will have no shaman, though, because the People need my father here."

Mary Carmen looked to me and her eyes were bright. I could have read her mind even if I hadn't possessed my special abilities. *Why not go with them?*

Aakif also seemed excited, sensing what we were thinking. He caught my eyes and nodded.

"Mary Carmen is a healer and I know of roots and herbs that heal. Aakif is a shipbuilder. You will need his skills if you are to live on the banks of a great lake. Would you allow us to come with you?"

"You are all welcome to join us," Winun'na said. "We are a small group and can use the help of skilled workers."

"I have my work, of course, and cannot join you," Van Leeuwenhoek said, "but it sounds like a grand and worthwhile venture to me."

John Indian came with the wagon. Tituba and Violet sat beside him. I spied Bronwyn wrapped in a blanket in the cart. We all surrounded the back of the wagon and I climbed in beside her. "How do you feel?"

Bronwyn clutched her head and I winced at the scar running up her forehead. "I'll be better soon, pet. Don't worry about me. The spirit is strong if the flesh is weak still. I'm a tough old bird."

From the shipyard, a seagull squawked as if on cue, which made all of us laugh. We told Tituba, John Indian, and Bronwyn what we were thinking. "Let's do it." Tituba was the first to agree.

"'O brave new world that has such people in it,'" Bronwyn quoted from *The Tempest*.

Aakif took my hand and I leaned against him. After all we had faced, we knew that whatever challenges the future held, we would be equal to them.

I no longer wanted to be a witch, and I didn't even want to live alone using my powers to make money in frivolous ways. Like Mother Kadiatu, like Bronwyn, like Mary Carmen, I wanted to be of help, to use what I could do to make things better.

Aakif would be with me and we would be all right. The words of the song I'd learned just over a year ago came to me.

The water is wide, I can-not cross o'er.
And neither have I the wings to fly.
Build me a boat that can carry two,
And both shall row, my true love and I.

"Tell your people we will be with them," I told Winun'na. "This world has grown too small for all of us. We're going to make a new one."